"I am from Hellas...from Greece."

"*You're* Greek?" That was the last thing he expected. He had met many Greek people or Americans of Greek ancestry. Most had fair, olive skin and straight, thick hair that was either light- or dark-brown. This woman was as blond as a towheaded toddler. And it was obvious from her pale lashes and skin that the color was natural.

A smile touched the corners of her mouth. "Yep."

"Do you have any more secrets to tell?"

"Oh, I have a few," she assured him with a mocking glance.

He was sure she must. He would enjoy getting to know each of them. If she would let him.

MELANIE PANAGIOTOPOULOS, born in Richmond, Virginia, currently resides in Athens, Greece, with her husband of nearly twenty-five years. They have two children. Melanie has done extensive research into the early-Christian and medieval periods of history and has published numerous articles on both subjects, something which is reflected in her books. To be where the early Christians and especially that great apostle to the Gentiles, Paul, worked and lived has inspired her greatly. She has spent many weekends with her family exploring little-known sites and many a winter morning sifting through dusty, but fantastic, books at some of the wonderful, old libraries Athens has to offer.

Books by Melanie Panagiotopoulos

HEARTSONG PRESENTS
HP217—Odyssey of Love
HP261—Race of Love
HP321—Fortress of Love
HP505—Happily Ever After

A Fairy-Tale Romance

Melanie Panagiotopoulos

Heartsong Presents

For my daughter, Sara, whose love of New York City inspired this story. Thanks for all your help and encouragement. You are the best!

A note from the author:
I love to hear from my readers! You may correspond with me by writing:

> **Melanie Panagiotopoulos**
> **Author Relations**
> **PO Box 719**
> **Uhrichsville, OH 44683**

ISBN 1-58660-922-X

A FAIRY TALE ROMANCE

Our mission is to publish and distribute inspirational products offering exceptional value and biblical encouragements to the masses.

All Scripture quotations, unless otherwise indicated, are taken from the HOLY BIBLE, NEW INTERNATIONAL VERSION®. NIV®. Copyright © 1973, 1978, 1984 by International Bible Society. Used by permission of Zondervan Publishing House. All rights reserved.

Note: *Handel's Messiah* (KJV) is taken from the arrangement conducted by Andrew Davis, music director of the Toronto Symphony. The symphony has often performed at Carnegie Hall in New York City.

All of the characters and events in this book are fictitious. Any resemblance to actual persons, living or dead, or to actual events is purely coincidental.

prologue

"He asked you to go to New York to become a model, Natalia? I don't know about this," said Martha Pappas, Natalia's much older sister.

Hopping up from the chair, Martha grabbed a sponge and began wiping the already immaculate kitchen table. She stopped, though, when their *baba* put out his hand to still her.

"Martha, sit down," he directed, his voice raspy but kind. He looked over the rim of his glasses at Natalia, his youngest child, and the only one of his six children who was adopted. "Tell us everything that happened. From the beginning."

Natalia nodded. Never had she been happier for the equilibrium of her father than at this moment. He was the clergy in the village of Kastro, so everyone referred to him as *Papouli*. But to his six children he was their beloved *baba*, and Natalia felt honored to be his daughter.

She reached for her glass of lemonade, took a sip, then started recounting the events that had brought her back unexpectedly to Kastro for the night. "Yesterday, feeling dissatisfied with the courses I'm following at school—" She paused and grimaced. "That's something else I have to talk to you about, *Baba*."

"Tell me about the modeling first," he instructed her gently.

She pushed her shoulder-length hair behind her ears. She was glad for his leading. "I decided to go up to the Areopagus, your favorite place in Athens." She referred to the hilltop location where the apostle Paul was purported to have preached to the Athenians in Acts, chapter seventeen. Her father went there whenever he visited the capital. "I was questioning whether I was indeed following the path God had laid out for me when a man came up to me and in a very nice way—and in English—asked if he might speak to me."

"English?" Martha asked, her brown eyes as round as basketballs.

Natalia nodded. "His name is Jasper Howard, and he is the president of Smile Modeling Agency in New York City."

"How can you be sure of this?" Martha asked. Natalia wasn't surprised. Martha had always been protective of her.

"Not only did he give me his business card"—she pointed to it on the table before her father—"but he removed from his wallet his passport, driver's license, and social-security card so I could see for myself that his identification proclaimed him to be Jasper Howard."

"And he wanted to talk to you about becoming a model for his agency?" her father prompted.

Natalia shrugged her shoulders. "That's right."

"What sort of modeling?" her father asked.

"Tasteful, fashionable clothing, nothing I might consider at all compromising."

"I don't know," Martha said again, and Natalia could hear the anxiety in her tone. "I've seen fashion shows on TV. I usually have to change the channel. They are"—she searched for the correct words—"well, you know."

"I know." Natalia reached out to comfort her. Martha was thirty-two years her senior; since their mother had died when Natalia was only ten, Martha was in many ways more a mother to Natalia than a sister. "That's why I told him the only way I could consider such a thing would be for him to come here and meet both of you, along with Allie and Stavros, who are Americans and know how things are done there." She referred to the village doctor and schoolteacher; doing so brought smiles to all three of their faces.

For at that moment they knew Stavros had taken Allie, who loved fairy tales, up to the castle that sat above the village to ask her to marry him. Allie had come to the village about a month ago and had changed the lives of Stavros and his daughter, Jeannie. Natalia, Martha, *Papouli*, and, in fact, the entire village knew that, if it was God's will, a romance was about to come to that deserving couple, and they would live happily ever after.

"But tell us," Martha asked in her quick way, "what did this Jasper Howard say when you asked him to come here to meet us?"

"He agreed to do so," Natalia replied.

"He did?" Her father's eyebrows shot upward. That seemed both to surprise and impress him.

"Yes."

"When?" Martha asked, jumping up from her chair.

Natalia pulled her back down. "Tomorrow. So calm down, Martha."

"Tell me." Her father leaned forward as he always did when he was about to ask something very important. "How would you feel about moving to New York?"

"That's the part about this whole thing that surprises me the most, *Baba*. Not only do I want to go, but somehow I almost feel pulled to the city. It's as if it's the path God wants me to take—the path He has laid out for me."

"You said you aren't happy with your courses at the fine arts school you are attending in Athens?" her father asked.

Natalia held her hands out in front of her, then let them drop onto her lap. Her father had given so much to send her to school in Athens, and she hated to disappoint him, but she knew she had to be honest. "It's not at all what I was expecting, *Baba*. It's too general and too abstract. It's wonderful for people who like that kind of art," she qualified, "but I don't. None of my classes has anything to do with fashion design." Ever since her mother had showed her how to hold a pencil and sew a straight seam, Natalia's hobby had been to draw and design dresses and make them into garments she could wear.

Her father was quiet for a moment, as if he were thinking over the matter. Suddenly he said, "Then perhaps you are meant to go to America at this time. I have always known God would somehow lead you back there."

Natalia had no idea about this. *"Baba?"*

"As you know," he began, "I feel certain that your birth mother was from the United States. That is why I have insisted upon your learning to speak English so well." She knew that at a great expense he had made sure her English was as perfect as it could be. Even Jasper Howard had commented on how fluently she spoke.

"But why do you feel this way, *Baba?* Not even the American embassy would recognize that I might be from America."

"The letter that was pinned to you from your birth mother said you were American. Plus you were dressed in that American-flag suit when *Baba* and *Mamma* found you at the bus station," Martha said. Natalia knew her sister still had the infant sleeper she had worn then; it was carefully wrapped in tissue paper tucked away in her dresser drawer. "And the blanket you were wrapped in was emblazoned with the American flag."

"But that still doesn't prove my nationality is American.

Anyone of any nationality could have written that letter or dressed me that way so I would be taken to America."

"True. That was the reasoning at the American embassy," her father admitted. "Plus, not a single American citizen had reported a missing baby." He sat back and settled his palms upon his skinny knees. "I don't know how to tell you why I feel as I do, Natalia. It's just something God has put into my heart." He looked at his daughter over the rim of his glasses. "And in the same way I have always known God would lead you back there someday, somehow, too." He lifted his hands then dropped them upon his knees again. "Maybe it is God's will that you search for your real parents."

"*Baba!*" She was aghast. "You and *Mamma* are my real parents!"

He smiled and patted her hand. "Yes, we are, and you have been such a blessing to us. I know your mother fought her illness and lived as long as she did only because she wanted to raise you—her beautiful and sweet-natured, fair-haired child—for as much time as she could."

"I loved her so much," Natalia whispered as she thought about the loving smiles and gentle voice of her mother. She would always remember her mother whenever the white jasmine flowers bloomed. That was her mother's scent.

"We all loved her," Martha said. "Still do."

"She was a very special woman," their *baba* agreed, and his eyes sparkled brightly with remembered happiness. It was a joyous look, but also the only time Natalia thought her father looked close to eighty years old. Even after eight years he missed his wife dearly.

He took a deep, settling breath. "Your mother was never angry at the woman who left you in the bus station. She always felt, as did I, that there must have been a reason, a good reason. Women do not give up their children without one. Maybe someday you will be led to her."

"That is not the reason why I want to go to America, *Baba*." Natalia wanted to make that clear. "I don't feel one way or the other about her, neither angry nor sad." She shrugged her shoulders. "I'm just glad I'm a part of *this* family."

"A very big part," Martha added quickly.

Natalia smiled over at her. "I don't know why I feel drawn to America—why something jumps in my soul at the idea of going—"

"God's leading, *agapi mou*—my love. God's leading." Her *baba* spoke with the authority of his calling. "Not only do you feel pulled to go, but also the way has been opened for you to go. I never would be able to afford the plane ticket for you, much less the other expenses involved with your living in New York City. If this *Jasper Howard*"—he spoke the unfamiliar name in a heavily accented tone which made Natalia smile—"is indeed the man he says he is, and if he can assure me you will be well taken care of, then I say go."

one

Six years later, New York City

Noel Sheffield glanced at his watch as he dashed from Seventh Avenue up Thirty-fourth Street on his way over to Fifth Avenue. It was an overcast day, and one might consider it gloomy with dusk falling earlier than usual. But the excitement of Christmas left no room for dreariness in the air. People were smiling and chatting like high school students at pep rallies do.

Noel glanced up at the pine that adorned the windows of Macy's Department Store and took a deep breath. Not only was it beginning to *look* a lot like Christmas, but it was beginning to *smell* like it too. Who would have imagined that midtown Manhattan could smell like a pine forest?

This was Noel's favorite time of the year. Judging from the expressions of people wrapped in brightly colored scarves and with smiles as big as the state of Alaska on their faces, he felt certain he wasn't alone in liking the season.

Christmastime in New York. He took a deep breath of satisfaction as the city he loved danced and pulsated to its own special holiday melody all around him. *What could be better?* he wondered as he stood at the traffic light at Herald Square where Broadway and Sixth intersected Thirty-fourth Street.

He glanced at his watch, and a sobering sigh of annoyance whistled through his teeth.

Of all days to be running late.

He had planned to leave the high school, where he worked as a guidance counselor, earlier today to ensure that he didn't miss his yearly rendezvous. Then a problem with one of his students had arisen. He sighed. Sixteen-year-old Rachel was running in the fast lane and was going to find herself in big trouble if she didn't listen to reason. But Noel knew it would have been easier for him—for anyone—to reason with a mouse than to try to persuade the girl of that fact.

The light changed. As Noel dodged holiday-garbed people coming toward him, he wondered again how he could make the girl understand that her lifestyle would lead only to heartache.

He took his position as counselor to the students at Westwood High School seriously. He felt that if he could catch a problem in a person and solve it at the high school level, it would be one less individual who would need the other profession for which he had trained: criminal lawyer.

But Noel didn't know if he had succeeded this time with Rachel or if he ever would. The girl was in trouble from a lack of good judgment. *Humph,* he thought. *A lack of judgment, period.* She had gotten herself into circumstances that needed much more wisdom than Noel could offer.

He drew in a deep breath.

But he was the girl's only chance. Her parents had paid thousands of dollars to private clinics and therapists in order to help her.

Nothing had worked.

As Noel had seen too often in the fast-paced world in which people lived today, busy lives precluded parents from doing anything personally for their children. That was the challenge of the whole situation. Most kids longed for their parents—at least one of them—to be around. After two years of counseling problem kids, Noel had decided they wanted quantity time with some of the overlauded quality time.

But it was what so few received.

To have their mom or dad in another part of the house with them—to be there for the two or three minutes they wanted to ask a question or be with the person who had made the commitment to raise them—meant a lot to children.

Noel had to give Rachel his best shot. Since she seemed to listen to him more than to anyone else, her parents had begged him to do whatever he could. He didn't want to let them down.

As he neared the famous shopping street, Fifth Avenue, the throngs of people were growing thicker and thicker. Even though Noel normally didn't mind rush-hour crowds—he found it exhilarating to be among so many people all in one spot at one moment and somewhere entirely different the next—it annoyed him today. He might miss the young woman with the dog.

The Rockefeller Center tree had been delivered during the previous night. Noel had seen it leave on the first part of its journey from his parents' home in New Jersey. He now had a tryst to keep with the tree *and* the woman.

For the past three years she had come to the center with her dog—a gorgeous German shepherd—at dusk on the day the tree was delivered. She always sat on the same bench in the Channel Garden and gazed up at the tree with a look of both yearning and joy. She had captured Noel's attention the first time he'd seen her. Noel knew she came to visit the tree on this day because he had done so ever since he was a little boy. His father used to bring him and tell him how *their* tree would one day stand at that "blessed spot."

Noel didn't know the woman and had never talked to her. He hoped to change that today. As he picked up his pace, his trench coat flapped out behind him like a flag.

He would speak to her this time in honor of *his* tree—the one he had grown up with—finally being the one to stand at the center, to grace the city of New York.

New York.

He glanced up at the decorated lamppost and flashed a smile at the red bow and Christmas flowers suspended from it. This city was the greatest place on earth, to Noel's way of thinking.

Especially at Christmas.

❧

"City sidewalks, busy sidewalks, dressed in holiday style. In the air there's a feeling of Christmas!" Natalia sang the refrain from one of her favorite holiday melodies softly as she walked with joyous steps down Fifth Avenue. Her four-and-a-half-year-old German shepherd, Prince, clipped by her side in perfect canine posture. With a plaid ribbon and bow of green and red tied around his neck, he was as well tailored in the Christmas way as the city of New York itself.

This was Natalia's favorite time of the year in the city. The hustle and bustle, the songs filling the atmosphere, the decorations, but mostly the way people seemed to smile at one another a little more as they passed each other brought warmth to her heart.

But as an arctic wind whipped around the corner of Central Park South and Fifth and caught her under her jaw, she gave a slight shiver and snuggled deeper into her down-filled ski parka.

"It's cold, Prince," she said.

He hunched his shoulders forward, looked up at her, and sent her his friendly, if lopsided, doggie grin.

Natalia laughed and wondered how anybody could be frightened of him. But people were, and she realized they had a right to be.

Prince would do anything for her, anything to protect her. He was as docile as a lamb—unless someone looked at her the wrong way. She smiled. She knew that fact made her *baba* and her sister Martha happy. Her *baba* might be a man of faith and trust God to look out for his youngest child in far-off New York, but he certainly didn't mind letting one of God's creatures help with the job.

She and Prince had returned the previous day from visiting her family in Kastro, Greece. As was her custom whenever she flew home, she had spent two glorious weeks there. She had moved away from the village six years ago, but not too much had changed, which of course was one of its main charms. Allie and Stavros, the village doctor and schoolteacher, had just added another child to their brood, making little Jeannie Andreas, who wasn't so little anymore, a very happy big sister. Jeannie loved her two brothers and her new baby sister to distraction. A smile curved Natalia's lips as she thought about Jeannie. The girl loved her stepmother, Allie, as dearly as any child could ever love a natural parent.

But that thought stole the rosiness the cold city day had put into Natalia's fair cheeks. Her *baba* had surprised her—shocked her even—on this trip home by almost insisting she search for her *own* natural mother. He hadn't said too much about it in the six years since she had left Kastro. But this time he had told her all that was in his heart; he felt that God wanted her to look for her biological mother or at least be open to finding her or to the possibility of her mother discovering her. The time was right, he said.

Natalia wasn't so sure.

She had done some research about people looking for biological parents; contrary to the stance of sentimentalists, it wasn't always so wonderful. Sometimes people didn't want to be found. Plus Natalia now had the added disadvantage of being what she called herself—a "genetic" celebrity. Because of the genes she had inherited from her unknown biological parents and the career she had chosen, her face was quite well known, at least in magazine layouts and on billboards.

Most models looked different in person than they did in magazines. Natalia was glad she was one of them. Further, she rarely wore makeup while going about the city, thus adding to her disguise. And one of the reasons she loved walking with Prince was because he was a good distraction. Most people looked at him more than they did her.

She smiled down at the dog.

Prince kept the tabloid photographers at bay too. They could snap pictures of other interesting people in New York, who didn't have a large dog with a mouth full of sharp teeth, rather than bother with her.

Jasper Howard had done more than make Natalia into a model. He had turned her into a modeling star. Not only was she famous in certain circles, but she had also made more money than she ever knew existed! And she gave large percentages of it away, something that made her feel happy. Her father had often preached that God required good stewardship of those He'd blessed materially. As Jesus taught in the parable of the talents, the more she gave, that much more she seemed to receive.

She wouldn't mind giving to her biological family should they be in need—she would be happy to do so. But she thought that she had to be careful because of the mystique behind being a model. Had her natural mother put her up for adoption it would have been different. But the woman had deserted her: She had left her in a bus station in a foreign land. If the woman had left her in an orphanage, at least Natalia would not have felt as uneasy about looking for her. But to be left in a bus station? What sort of woman did that?

"The desperate kind," a voice seemed to answer her. *"A woman desperate in a way you have never had to experience—because of her actions."*

Natalia sighed.

She didn't know what to do. The truth was, her birth mother might have deserted her, but no one could have asked for a better set of parents than the ones who had loved her for much longer than she could remember. Her adoptive mother died when Natalia was only ten, but that didn't take away the joy she had in being that lovely woman's daughter.

The sound of a Volunteer of America Santa ringing his Christmas bell drew her attention. He was a joyous figure in red splashed against the backdrop of the city. Natalia reached into her pocket for some bills.

"Merry Christmas!" she said as she dropped them into the bucket.

"Ho, ho, ho," he sang out and rang his bell loudly. "Merry Christmas to you too, young lady. And many thanks."

Nodding to him she walked on, a warm feeling of hope and good cheer washing over her. She looked up at the green lamppost above her. Its artful arrangement of bows and poinsettias made her smile widen.

She loved New York.

Loved it passionately.

She wouldn't want to live anywhere else.

But she knew that having the means to live in a nice area of the city meant she had a responsibility to give back the blessings.

That thought inevitably returned her to her father's views on searching for her biological mother. His opinion was too wise to ignore. She breathed a prayer into her plaid, cashmere scarf, adding to the many she had said while flying the previous day across the Atlantic. "Dear Lord, Your will be done in this matter, please. If You want my natural mother and me to find one another, so be it." She paused and smiled as a professional dog walker handling seven dogs passed her. "But if my natural mother could now be a Christian, that would really help." With that, she let go of the thoughts that had been plaguing her about her biological parentage. She wanted only to enjoy this very special moment of being back in New York City.

Natalia was heading for the tree at Rockefeller Center. She'd heard from her doorman, Roswell Lincoln, that it had been delivered during the night. It had become her personal tradition to see the tree before it was decorated. She loved the trees when five miles' worth of lights graced their branches, but there was something special about seeing them in their almost-natural state.

The Walk sign flashed on in yellow letters. She tightened her grip on Prince's lead, then motioned the dog forward and crossed the intersection. Glancing to her right, past the horse-drawn carriages and the Pulitzer Fountain ringed with twinkle lights, she saw the towers of the Plaza Hotel.

Natalia smiled as she remembered the first time she had walked into that building, which was styled after a French château. It hadn't been dressed and waiting for the arrival of Christmas as it was now, sparkling in holiday adornment, with lights aglow along its towers and bunting festively arrayed across its entrance awning. But it had still seemed like something out of a storybook to her. Jasper Howard had rented a suite of rooms for her there upon her arrival from Kastro.

She'd felt like a little girl who had just entered a fairyland castle. But it wasn't a fortress-type castle like the one of thick stones and buttressed walls she had played upon in Kastro; rather it was like a palace where kings and queens might live in splendor. With all that velvet and mahogany, crystal and gold, it was opulent and exquisite with rich detailing and an elegance that Natalia had never experienced before. She was thankful Jasper's wife, Janet, had come to meet her there. Taking one look at Natalia's tired and flabbergasted face, she had understood that the Plaza was not the place for a young woman fresh from a Greek mountain village to be staying in on her own.

Janet had immediately invited Natalia into their spacious apartment, where she had stayed like a beloved daughter for nearly a year. Natalia now had her own apartment in the same building on the Upper East Side and was still very close to Janet and Jasper. They were her mentors, her friends, but, most of all, her sister and brother in the Lord. They had wanted her to stay with them longer, but when the three-bedroom apartment came up for sale she knew it was time for her to move.

She loved her apartment. Although it was bigger than what she needed, it was the one area in her life where she had splurged and felt no guilt in doing so. Because of it, her numerous brothers and sisters—but mostly Martha, the sister she was closest to—and her father had often come to visit her. It never failed to amaze her father that he could look out the window and see a good portion of the trees that filled Central Park. He took daily walks in the park whenever he came. On her most recent trip home, Natalia was pleased to see that, at eighty-five years of age, he hadn't changed at all in the six months since she had last seen him. She felt certain the final verse in Psalm 91, " 'With long life will I satisfy him and show him my salvation,' " applied to her dear *baba*. Even though he was semiretired, he was still the village clergy, still as strong as he had been ten years earlier, and still helping others, both physically and spiritually.

Prince looked up at her as he came to a stop at the corner of Fifth and Fifty-eighth. She reached down, adjusted his collar, and rubbed his neck beneath it.

"Good boy," she whispered to him and smiled. Prince was trained never to cross a street without first stopping to check for traffic. She gave the command for them to continue and looked up at the sophisticated decorations at Bergdorf Goodman. Holiday wreaths adorned every window of the building.

But it was the giant snowflake suspended high over Fifth and Fifty-seventh she was searching for now. She gave a light laugh when she saw it lit resplendently above the avenue, then spoke to her dog.

"I love snow, but I'm sure glad snowflakes aren't really that big." She patted the dog's thick woolly fur. "Even you would have a problem walking through the amount of snow such flakes would produce, dear Prince."

Crossing over Fifty-seventh Street, she pushed up her sleeve and glanced at her watch. It read 4:25. She increased her pace. If she didn't hurry, she wouldn't make it to Rockefeller Center until too late. It had been her tradition the last few years to see the newly arrived tree as day faded into night.

But even more important she wanted to get there in time to see the handsome man who had filled so many of her romantic thoughts during the last three years.

Because of her work and studies, but mainly because she hadn't met anyone she wanted to know better, Natalia had shied away from dating during the years she had been in New York. But something about that unknown stranger tugged at her.

She had first seen him three years ago.

He was tall and dark, with a ruggedly handsome appearance, and she had noticed him standing by the corner of the South Promenade that first year gazing at the tree with a sort of longing and thoughtfulness, which had touched her heart. The strangest thing, though she would never admit it to another living soul, was that he looked like the man she had dreamed about ever since she was a little girl, the man she knew God would someday bring into her life and with whom she would spend the rest of her life. It wasn't that he was so handsome—those kind of men could be found anywhere— rather, it was an illusive *something* that drew her to him.

She had found herself thinking about who he might be, what he did, and what he believed at strange times through- out the years. She supposed it was because she didn't want to date, and thoughts about him were safe.

But when she saw him again last year, not only on this day but also at the Macy's Thanksgiving Day parade and again at the Lincoln Center's annual performance of the *Nutcracker* ballet, she had thought she'd conjured him up. New York was a large city, and it was rare to meet the same people at various locations.

But with all the longing of a woman who loved fairy tales, she hoped she might see him again today. He could easily be her "Prince Charming."

She shook her head at the silly notion and, reaching down, rubbed her fingers across the velvety softness of her dog's ears. "You're my only Prince, aren't you, Boy?"

The dog looked up at her with that look in his eyes he sometimes got that made her think he understood her perfectly. Giving a little laugh, she said, "Never mind," and turned back to the avenue upon which they walked.

Even though it was barely mid-November the sounds of Christmas filled the air—bells, music, laughter. Some people said it was too early, too commercial. Natalia didn't agree.

Maybe it was commercial, and perhaps many people didn't allot enough time to think about the true meaning of Christmas. But Natalia saw it all as being in honor of the Babe who had been born so long ago. *Well, maybe not all,* she conceded as a street vendor called out to everyone to buy his "cheap, barking, 'dog' toy." But the Babe born in Bethlehem was the original idea behind the celebration of Christmas. Natalia felt that the so-called Christmas feeling or spirit so many people loved at this time drew many to look again at the birth of Jesus.

Maybe some of the people she passed on the busy street with their holiday bags and Christmas colors adorning them didn't have any insight into the "mystery that has been kept hidden for ages and generations," until Christ's arrival. But perhaps the celebration of Christmas appealed to so many because something stirred within them at this time, something that made each person somehow know a mystery had been made known to mankind upon Christ's birth. She wasn't sure, of course. But that's what she thought.

She looked around her as her steps carried her farther down the world-famous shopping avenue. It was festooned with red and green and lit in a Christmassy way. As she crossed one street after another she remembered how her father had taught her that Christmas, from the beginning of its observance in A.D. 354, was more for nonbelievers to draw close to Christ than for believers. With so many Christmas scenes all around her, she believed it was probably still so.

The Gothic spires of the cathedral on the next block down and across the street caught Natalia's gaze. As a structure built to honor the Prince of Peace, it was superb. When its construction was first considered back in the mid-1800s, no one could imagine how the city of New York would grow up around it. Until skyscrapers appeared in the 1930s, she had read that the 330-foot spires of St. Patrick's Cathedral had towered above the city and had been part of its skyline even then.

It was counted as one of the largest cathedrals in the world, and, throughout the last six years, Natalia had often found solace and peace within its welcoming walls. People representing the entire world might be passing by its huge bronze doors, but the peace and tranquillity she found in that Gothic structure made it one of her favorite places in the city. It didn't matter to her that it wasn't a church of her persuasion. What counted was who was honored and loved there: Jesus, God's Son.

She glanced up at the sky.

It was dusk now. *Perfect for seeing the tree,* she thought.

She walked onto the North Promenade and gasped.

It was like a fairy world.

In the dusky mistiness of the late autumn evening, the horn-blowing ensemble of wire-sculpted angels was aglow, reminiscent of those actual angels that had heralded the birth of Christ so long ago. The stars that twinkled around them made them seem as if they were part of the heavenly host.

And the tree. . .

Natalia stood in awe of the Norway spruce. It was bigger and fuller than any she had seen before. Framed by the seventy stories of the General Electric Building behind it, the ice rink and Channel Garden before it, the tree stood, majestic and beautiful, a monument to the wonder of God's work on the third day of creation.

She repeated softly the words in Genesis as she gazed at the tree's regal beauty: " 'Then God said, "Let the land produce vegetation: seed-bearing plants and trees on the land that bear fruit with seed in it, according to their various kind." ' "

In this city of concrete and steel, the tree was like an oasis, a small selection of nature that God, the bestower of everything good and wonderful, gives life to and shares with His creation on earth. The workmen who had built the center back in the early 1930s during the depression had brought the first Christmas tree here, starting a yearly tradition. Meant to gladden their spirits, as well as the spirits of all those who passed by and saw it, similar trees had done so for more than six decades.

Natalia inhaled a deep breath of air. The tree's limbs still held their natural clean fragrance. This was another reason she looked forward to seeing the tree upon its arrival. By tomorrow it would no longer smell so much like the country. Having grown up in the mountains of Greece, Natalia almost craved the fresh aroma.

She walked over to one of the benches situated beneath an angel and sat down.

She knew that once the tree was lit she wouldn't find a place to sit at this time of day. That was another reason she always came now. And she wanted to watch the faces of the people as they rushed along Fifth Avenue and see the child-like brightening that filled their faces when they spied the tree in its place.

A lovely representative of the Tree of Life and the redemptive work of Jesus Christ, the Christmas tree in its celebrated place would catch most by surprise. Young and old, rich and poor, people from all over the world would pause for a moment on their journey through life that day and look up at the tree. Without fail, a dreamy sort of smile would soften the lines of their faces, as if the sight of it would, for a moment, cause them to forget their worries and cares.

The tree proclaimed the arrival of the Christmas season in New York City. Christ's incarnate birth, which enabled all who believed to become children of God through adoption, would soon be celebrated once more.

And that made Christmas-loving Natalia very happy.

She scanned the Channel Garden. The only thing that would make her woman's heart happier would be to see the prince of her romantic daydreams.

two

Noel turned the corner of the South Promenade next to the French Building. Before he even looked up at the tree, he searched for the woman he had hoped to see again this year.

He immediately spied her sitting on a bench opposite the fountains, looking like an angel in a forest of celestial beings. He skidded to a halt.

Her head was uncovered, and her hair, as golden as the radiant beings that surrounded her, glowed luminously in the cozy duskiness. She was gazing upward toward the ninety-foot tree, but to Noel it was as if she were looking at much more than the tree he had played upon and beneath as a child. The tilt of her profile made her seem as though she were trying to see into her future, contemplating what it might hold. He wished it to be one full of sunshine and beauty—and him.

Usually he would pause for a few minutes, wondering if the next year his tree would finally stand in this special place, and send covert glances in the girl's direction.

But this year everything was different.

This year *his* tree—one of the most beautiful, most symmetrical, and most cherished trees in the world—was in the place it had been marked to grace since Noel's grandfather had witnessed the first tree placed in Rockefeller Center in 1931. When six of the ten Norway spruces planted at the same time as this one had succumbed to last winter's severity, his parents decided to let this year be its turn at the center. The official gardener of the Rockefeller Center, who had kept his professional eye on the tree during the last twenty years, agreed it was the right decision. It was very old and might not make it through another hard New England winter.

And because of his tree Noel wasn't going to wonder about the girl any longer; he was going to go over and talk to her.

With long strides he let his feet carry him the short distance to the North Promenade.

The dog was the first to notice him. He turned his noble head with his finely chiseled jaw in Noel's direction. Noel casually looked into the dog's eyes. From growing up with German shepherds he sensed this one had to have been well treated and was probably one of the more gentle—unless his mistress had a need. Noel knew he didn't need to fear him. Seeming to come to the same decision about him, the dog's long, feathery tail started to brush softly against the ground, and Noel was glad to be recognized as a friend. Feeling the dog's movement, the girl turned.

She looked up at Noel.

Their gazes met.

Her blue eyes blinked.

His blue eyes blinked back.

Vitality and excitement seemed to flow through every line of her. He had thought she was beautiful when glancing at her from a distance. But from only about eight feet away and looking directly at her, with her soul seeming to shine through her eyes, she carried Noel's breath away on a cloud of enchanting white.

Golden and light, blue and bright, she fit in perfectly with the twelve sculpted Clarebout angels that surrounded her. If he didn't know better, he would say she was one too, of the highest order. He hoped she wasn't, though. He didn't want to fall in love with an angel.

He wanted to fall in love with a woman.

With this woman.

And as superficial as it might sound, even to him, he knew he was already in love with her, or at least he was the closest he had ever been to that elusive emotion. Something about her, something almost familiar in her eyes—a certain light—made him love her when their gazes came together in an embrace of mutual interest. At that moment their souls seemed to merge and sing like a celestial host proclaiming something wonderful and right. Noel felt an explosion within his head as bright with lights as his tree would soon be, and even more he felt as if he were the happy prince in a wonderful fairy tale.

As strange as it might sound for a healthy, red-blooded American male to admit, Noel loved fairy tales now as much as he did when he was a little boy, especially those in which the guy and the girl lived happily ever after. He only hoped he might soon be living one with this remarkably beautiful girl who caught his interest and wouldn't let go. Her beauty encompassed much more than the fine placement of her features upon the planes of her face; rather, it reached out and touched the core of him.

≈

When Natalia looked up and saw the man she had wondered about during the last few years before her, she blinked, thinking her recent thoughts about him had conjured him up.

His eyes were blue, something that surprised her. With such dark hair she had expected brown. But she wasn't disappointed.

Who could be? They were the warm and restful blue of the Grecian sky in summertime. Besides, she didn't think that anything about him could disappoint her at this moment. His appearance was everything she could ever want in a man. A part of her almost didn't want to know him any further; he was perfect now.

As he nodded his head toward Prince, she knew he was going to speak. She braced herself for what he might say, for what might come out and shatter the illusion she'd built. She hoped he wouldn't say anything that might turn her prince into a toad.

❧

Noel, indifferent to the impression he created, pointed to the dog and said, "He's a magnificent beast."

Her head dipped slightly in response. Scratching behind her dog's ears, she said, "I'm glad you like him."

"What's his name?"

She smiled up at him, an almost self-conscious sort of smile. "Promise not to laugh."

His mouth quirked in a humorous line. She sounded like one of his students admitting to an embarrassing occurrence. "I promise."

"Prince Charming."

In light of his thoughts a moment earlier, Noel wouldn't have laughed even if she hadn't asked him not to. "I like it."

"Really?"

"I guess you must like fairy tales then."

"I grew up on them. Love them," she admitted quickly. "Romantic movies too."

"Is that why you come here to see the tree year after year on the day it arrives? Because it brings a little fairy-tale wonder to New York?" He could tell his observation had startled her from the way her eyes widened.

He felt bad for being so blunt. But now that he had finally talked to her, he wasn't going to play games. She didn't know him any more than she knew the millions of people walking the streets of New York, and she might think it strange if, after even a few minutes of talking, he told her he'd seen her before. He didn't want her to think he'd been stalking her.

After a short moment her pale brows lifted. Nodding in the direction of where he usually stood leaning against the French Building, she returned, "Is it why you come too?"

Now it was his turn to be taken aback. His mouth narrowed. He hadn't expected that. But the fact she admitted to it told him something about her character. She was honest. Not a game player.

He liked that—a lot.

Most of the women he had met during the last few years played the male-female game. That was the reason he hadn't formed a lasting relationship, even though it was something he desired.

"I love the holiday season," he answered. He was glad for his training that enabled him to think about several things while answering something entirely different. "Perhaps because the city does take on a fairy-tale type appearance during the Christmas season."

"I agree. Except I like to think of it as a God tale," she said.

Her description of the Christmas season stunned Noel. His parents often compared the season to being a God tale rather than a fairy tale. He had never heard anybody else describe it like that. It unnerved him.

"Christ's birth is proclaimed around the city, around the

world," she continued, oblivious to the sensation her words brought to him, "in its decorations, lights, and pageantry. It's really nice."

Noel knew then why she had seemed familiar to him. The bright, open look in her eyes, one of wholesomeness, forth-rightness, and an otherworldly sort of wisdom, was similar to what he often saw in his parents' eyes. She had to be a Christian as they were, making Christ the center of their lives. It had always bothered Noel a bit concerning his parents—he had a thing about fanatics of any kind—but he didn't mind the trait in this girl at all.

In fact, somehow, it made her seem even better to him.

Because of his parents he had a good idea what sort of character she would have and, as important, wouldn't have.

It was as if he held a secret knowledge about her.

He liked that.

He had rejected his parents' all-encompassing religious lifestyle, but he found he could accept it in her.

This was quite an ironic revelation for Noel.

❧

Natalia stopped speaking.

Sometime in their conversation she had lost him. She wondered if it was her description of the Christmas season in New York City being a God tale rather than a fairy tale. She felt sad to think this might prove a stumbling block to their getting to know each other better, but she didn't regret saying it. It broke her heart to see the beauty of the true story behind Christmas turned into a multitude of fairy tales. Loving fairy tales as she did, she believed they definitely had their place. Didn't she hope for her own Prince Charming someday? But he would have to know God personally and would have to believe that Truth came into the world the day God came to earth as a human baby.

"I'm sorry," he said. Natalia noticed his strong, square-cut chin lift a fraction of an inch. "My parents have always described this season that way."

She felt her pulse pick up its rhythm. Could this man she had thought about so often during the last few years be a believer? Motioning to the bench, she did something she had never done before. "Would you like to sit down?" Her sister's teaching on safety in the big city had been deeply ingrained in her, and she had always been careful about strangers.

"Thanks," he said, lowering his tall frame with an easy grace onto the bench. She wasn't surprised when Prince stood, instinctively putting himself between her and the man.

"Hey, Prince Charming." The man slowly extended the back of his hand for the dog to sniff. "You're a handsome fellow."

The dog stood in perfect German-shepherd pose, with his hind legs stretched back, his chest out, and his head held high. Natalia laughed. "Careful—he's already too vain."

The man turned his head to get a good look at the dog's lines. "He must come from championship stock."

"Sit, Prince," she commanded the dog, who promptly obeyed. "Yes, his grandfather was the world champion a few years ago." She leaned down and nuzzled her nose against the velvety smoothness of her dog's ears. "But I don't show him. He was a gift and is champion enough for me without the ribbons. You know about German shepherds?"

"I grew up with them," he returned. "My parents still have two. Ten-year-old Laddie and his son, Harry."

Yes, we have a love of dogs in common, she thought. That was nice, especially if. . .they should get to know one another better. "I hope you don't mind my asking, but are your parents Christians?"

A smile tugged at the corners of his mouth. "I don't think anybody could be any more so."

She laughed, a merry musical sound that expressed how happy his response made her. "Well, I doubt they feel that way. Being a Christian is a work in progress. I don't think any Christian feels he or she is living the Christian life perfectly." She laughed again. "No one is perfect except Christ."

"I think they would agree with you."

"And you?" Her gaze narrowed. She wanted to know.

He took another deep breath. "I'm not sure. I guess I haven't wanted to give my parents' beliefs a chance because"—he flashed that endearing grin again, but with a touch of remorse to it—"it's what *they* believe."

She'd heard of that before. Janet and Jasper had had a similar experience with their oldest son—a man now in his forties—until he met a special woman of faith. Natalia decided it was better not to comment.

His response wasn't what she had hoped it would be, nor was it entirely negative. He might be open to learning *if,* like Janet and Jasper's oldest son, he had someone other than his parents to show him the way.

"So, tell me, do you believe in fairy tales?" he asked, obviously redirecting the conversation back to their original discussion.

"Sure, I do. I've seen them come true often enough."

Noel turned his head to the side. "You mean with real princes and princesses?"

"No. Between a doctor and a schoolteacher. Between the president of a modeling agency and a museum director.

And, well, between my own father and mother." She shrugged her shoulders. "Simple people like that."

He chuckled. "I don't think there's anything simple about being a doctor or a schoolteacher or any of those things. And for a child to think of her parents' marriage as a fairy-tale romance must mean you have remarkable parents."

"Very."

"I do too," he quickly returned and smiled at her. She smiled back. It was as if he knew what a gift his parents had given him, as her parents had given her: a family unit in which a child could find that special place of peace and security and love.

In this age of divorce and light romantic flings, his words made Natalia's heart sing. They had something basic and important in common: parents who loved one another and who loved God. She nodded her head, but as the star on the top of the tree flicked on—the tree's only light—and caught the corner of her eye, she exclaimed, "Oh, look! Isn't it beautiful?"

❧

Noel turned his gaze toward the tree.

Seeing his tree at this famous plaza and finally meeting the young woman made him happy in a way he hadn't been since he was a child on Christmas morning and beheld the gifts under the tree for him. With her profile silhouetted before the Rockefeller tree he whispered out, "Beautiful."

Both the girl and the conifer were.

And no matter what the future might hold for them, this moment would be one of his most cherished memories.

"This night is almost more thrilling than the tree-lighting ceremony. We are mostly alone"—she waved her arm toward the heralding angels and laughed—"except for our heavenly host, of course, and we have the expectation of the coming holiday season before us."

"I like this time of the year more than any other," Noel admitted. He didn't know why, but the lights and happy music, the ringing bells and merry decorations, seemed to make something within him jump to life.

"I think hearts are more open to God's truth at this time of the year than at any other. Maybe"—she looked shyly toward him—"that's what you feel." She motioned toward the people rushing along the avenue in buses, taxis, and cars; on roller blades, scooters, and feet. "Perhaps everyone does."

"The spirit of Christmas," Noel whispered, thinking that explained what she described.

She looked at him in a sort of contemplative way, as if she wasn't sure she should speak her thoughts.

"Tell me," he prompted.

Her smile widened. "Are you sure? I have quite strong opinions about things, and once I get started—"

"I'd like to hear them," he interrupted. He wanted to know everything she thought, everything she believed. He'd like to spend a lifetime learning.

Amusement glinted in her eyes. "Okay," she said and twisted a strand of golden hair behind her ear. "Well, did you know that 'the spirit of Christmas' is actually an expression from the Middle Ages that describes a jovial medieval figure?"

"Really? I had no idea. If I had thought about it, I would have said it came from the pen of Charles Dickens."

"I know. But it was around long before he was. And there is a big difference between the 'spirit of Christmas' and that of God's Spirit touching people's hearts in a personal way. God is real. Not an invention of man."

His parents might have said the same thing to him in the past, but he hadn't paid attention. He found himself wanting to pay attention to this golden-haired woman with perfect features. "Go on." He motioned for her to continue. He liked watching her lips curve as she spoke.

"Are you sure? As I said, I have a lot of thoughts about these things." She laughed, a light tinkling sound that reminded Noel of fine crystal touched by the wind.

"I want to hear what you believe." He really did. She was a thinker. He was glad she was so much more than a pretty face. It didn't surprise him.

"Well, I think God's Holy Spirit can more easily touch the hearts of people now. Christmas makes people wonder a little more than they normally do about God coming to earth as a little baby." She pointed behind them to the statues of the heralding angels.

Could that be the reason I love Christmas so much? Noel wondered. It was an interesting thought, but he doubted that was it. To believe in the message of Christmas, a person had to believe God did, in fact, come to earth as a baby. He wasn't so sure about that. It seemed like a nice fairy tale. But that was all. He believed in God and thought Jesus had been a remarkable man.

But God born as a human baby?

He wasn't going to tell this young woman that now, though. It wasn't the time or the place. And more than anything he wanted to meet her again, and he doubted—

His thoughts ground to a halt as she reached for her dog's lead and stood. "You're going?" he asked.

Nodding, she motioned for Prince to take his correct place beside her left heel. She glanced at her watch. "I have to."

He jumped up. "Wait—I mean—" He looked down. The dog watched him carefully, without his tail wagging. Noel knew German shepherds well enough to know he'd stood too suddenly for the dog's liking. "I'd like to see you again."

The girl reached down and patted the dog between his ears, assuring him all was well. She flashed her bright and lovely smile. "I have a feeling we'll meet again next year right here."

"I'd like to see you before then." *And learn what you think about and believe,* he wanted to say. Instead he watched as her gaze roamed over his face; something in the way she looked at him told him she wanted to see him sooner too.

"I'll be at the Macy's Thanksgiving Day parade," she offered.

He grimaced. "You and several million others."

She smiled at the truth of that statement. "Well, I'll be at Herald Square." She went a step further and offered him her exact location before she looked up at the tree one more time. "It was special to talk to you finally." He wondered if she could hear his heart pound louder at her admission.

"Kind of like a fairy tale," he said.

She flashed him a high-wattage smile of agreement and, giving a command to Prince, turned and walked through the Channel Garden, around the corner, and out of sight. It was only as he watched the dog's feathery tale disappear around the edge of the building that Noel realized he hadn't asked her for her name.

He banged the heel of his hand against his forehead and laughed. There had to be poetic irony in that. The study of names was one of his favorite hobbies, and he'd even written a book titled *What's in a Name?* It had recently made the *New York Times* best-seller list. He turned and walked in the direction of his tree. For a few days more she would have to be the girl with the dog who visited the tree on the day of its arrival.

But that didn't matter. He had something more important than her name; he had a glimpse of the soul her beautiful exterior housed. And he was beginning to think it was more attractive than her appearance—he glanced in the direction she had walked—if that were possible.

He doubted that Cinderella or Sleeping Beauty could have had souls any nicer than his very own fairy-tale princess.

Princess, he mused, gazing at his tree. He wondered if her name might be Sara. It meant 'Princess.'

"Could very well be," he muttered to himself. He felt better than he had in a long time. He could almost break into Gene Kelly's rendition of "Singin' in the Rain" and click his heels at any moment. He bowed to a family of tourists who looked at him as if he were the perfect specimen of one of those "crazy" New Yorkers they had heard about, one who walked along the streets talking to himself.

But Noel knew he *was* crazy.

Crazy in love with a woman he had only talked to once, a woman he would meet at Herald Square in a little over a week.

Noel did click his heels.

And the tourists practically ran away from him.

three

Less than a week later he turned from a side street onto Fifth Avenue and saw her. She was standing in line with Prince to see the Christmas windows unveiled at a famous department store. Noel felt as if he were living a fairy tale.

What were the chances of their running into one another like this in New York City? Slim to none, he knew. Noel didn't believe in chance or destiny or that New Age mumbo jumbo. Enough of what his parents believed had rubbed off on him to trust that God had a hand in directing the steps of people. Noel liked the way his steps had been pointed this day.

The woman who had occupied much of his thoughts was standing not far from the end of the line. He walked up to her. As at the Rockefeller Center, the dog noticed him first. Noel was glad to see her canine friend did his job so well.

"Hi, Prince," he greeted the dog, putting his hand out for him to sniff it. The woman turned to him. Pleasure covered the smooth lines of her face. He was glad to see it. He knew his own face had to be wearing the same emotion.

"Hi!" she exclaimed. Noel felt as if the joy of the season were expressed in the brightness of her gaze. "This is a nice surprise!"

"Nice surprise." Something jumped inside Noel at her words. "I couldn't agree more."

"What are you doing here?" she asked as if he were an old friend and not a person whose name she didn't know.

He motioned to his camera, then toward the decorated windows before them. "I understand each one resembles a Victorian-dollhouse set this year. My mother loves dollhouses and collects and makes them, so I wanted to take some shots for her."

The girl's mouth dropped open as she touched her chest. "I collect dollhouses too! That's why I've come today, even though"—she hiked up the sleeve of her coat to check her watch—"I don't have the time."

He wondered what she did to make her so pressed, but he only said, "I'll have to get you together with my mother. She has several scattered around her home. She's built Victorian homes herself—one from a kit and the other from scratch, plus another modeled after her own home, also from scratch."

"Really!" Her eyes widened in appreciation of the work that went into making three houses. "That's impressive. I've only just finished building my first Victorian. And that from a kit," she said. "I would love to see them. Does she live here in Manhattan?"

"She used to, but now my parents live in a big old home with lots of land around them in New Jersey." It was actually a mansion, one that had been in Noel's family for several generations. But he didn't tell the girl that.

"Hey, Buster," a man with a heavy Queens accent who had a little girl by his side called out to Noel from about three places behind them. "If you're goin' to see the windows you have to move to the back of the line. No line breakin' allowed."

Grimacing, Noel turned to the man. "Sorry. I just ran into—"

"Yeah, yeah. I've heard that story before," the man said without giving Noel the chance to explain.

Noel stiffened at the uncalled-for accusation, but sensing

the woman's soft touch on his arm, he swallowed the retort he'd been about to make.

"Let's move to the end of the line," she urged him and, not waiting for his reply, motioned for Prince to turn around.

"But you said you were in a hurry—"

She shook her head. "It doesn't matter. We're only about"—she glanced toward the end—"thirty places from the rear anyway. If it makes that man happy, then why not? Maybe he's had a hard day. It's an easy way to show him people care about him, even people he doesn't know."

If Noel hadn't already thought she was a remarkable woman, he would now. She seemed to be wise in a way that was far beyond her years.

And—her appearance aside—he understood why he was already in love with her.

As they walked back, the belligerent man's gaze followed them in surprise. Noel noticed that his anger seemed to evaporate off his broad shoulders like snow under the shining sun. "Hey—thanks. If only more people were so fair."

The woman smiled over at him with a look that could have melted the largest iceberg in the arctic. It definitely warmed the man's disposition. He stared at her, with his mouth hanging open and his eyes as round as saucers, and Noel guessed he was probably falling in love with her as well.

"I wonder," Noel said as they took their place at the end of the line, "how much better that stranger's day will be because you agreed to move back." Her action wasn't too unusual for Noel. He had seen his parents do things like that many times. But never someone near his own age. "You didn't have to move back with me."

"I wanted to," she replied quickly. Noel felt gladness fill his heart over her admission. Did he dare suppose she wanted to know him as much as he wanted to know her?

She smiled. "I know we weren't in the wrong. I could have come early and saved a place in line for both of us." Noel liked the way that sounded. That would mean they were a couple, or at least friends. "But," she said, shrugging her slender shoulders, "my father always told me if I could do something to calm another person, especially with such a little cost as this, a place in a line"—she shrugged her shoulders again, a cute habit Noel was beginning to associate with her—"then why not? Who knows what's going on in that man's life?"

"Sounds as if you have a wise father."

"I do," she agreed as they took short steps forward to the display. "So tell me," she said, changing the subject, "where in New Jersey do your parents live?"

"Madison."

Her brows came together thoughtfully. "I'm not sure where that is. I haven't seen much of New Jersey, but I hear it's beautiful." She flashed her smile and gave her tinkling little laugh. "Much more than the New Jersey Turnpike, that is."

He chuckled in agreement. Most people thought New Jersey looked like the industrial area that followed the turnpike across its length, not realizing the state was one of the prettiest on the East Coast. "That it is. But, shh," he said, leaning toward her. At her scent—clean and fresh like powder on a baby's skin—his senses reeled, and he took a hasty step back to clear his head. "It's one of the best-kept secrets in that area."

"Then I won't tell," she said in a conspiratorial way. Craning her neck toward the first window whose brightly lit display was becoming visible, she said, "Now you know one of my favorite hobbies is collecting and building dollhouses." She turned to him. "How about you? Do you have a hobby?" In the chill of the evening her frosted breath mingled with his like an enchanting cloud of togetherness. Snappy holiday songs piped out onto the street from the department store helped turn the moment into a great Christmassy one. *"It's that time of year, when the world seems to say. . .Merry Christmas!"* And Noel wanted to lean toward the woman who, because of the crowds, was standing as close to him as a girlfriend might and kiss her.

But, of course, he didn't. At even the slightest start Prince might grab his leg, but, even more importantly, Noel knew it wouldn't be right.

He stood up straight and fought to remember her question. His hobby? "Names," he managed to reply. He was pleased he could get the word past his throat. He felt as tense as the tightest setting on a windup toy.

She blinked back at him in confusion. "Names?"

He nodded his head. "I enjoy onomastics."

"Onoma—" She paused. Then, as if a light had suddenly switched on, she exclaimed, "You mean you like the study of names?"

Now he was the one to be surprised. "I'm impressed." He was. Most thought onomastics had something to do with gymnastics.

"Don't be." She laughed, a sound that to Noel sounded like the bells of Christmas ringing out over the wintry world. She shook her head and explained. *"Onoma* is the Greek word for 'name.' If you know elementary Greek, it's easy. *Onoma* is, of course, one of the first words a person learns. *Ti enia to onoma sou?*—'What is your name?' "

To say he was astonished would be to put it mildly. He was

flabbergasted. He was normally the one explaining the history of a word to another. "How do you know Greek?"

She touched her gloved hand to her heart and, in a way he could only describe as proud, replied, "I am from Hellas. . .from Greece."

"*You're* Greek?" That was the last thing he expected. He had met many Greek people or Americans of Greek ancestry. Most had fair, olive skin and straight, thick hair that was either light- or dark-brown. This woman was as blond as a towheaded toddler. And it was obvious from her pale lashes and skin that the color was natural.

A smile touched the corners of her mouth. "Yep."

"Do you have any more secrets to tell?"

"Oh, I have a few," she assured him with a mocking glance.

He was sure she must. He would enjoy getting to know each of them. If she would let him. "Well, how do you speak English so well?"

"Most people in Greece speak English—actually, several foreign languages. But, for personal reasons, it was important to my father that I learn to speak English well with as little accent as possible." Now, as he listened to her carefully, he could hear a slight difference to the way she pronounced words. She softened the English language. Not an accent exactly, but more a treat for his ears, a caress he rejoiced in hearing. "I had lessons from a very young age."

"Greece. . .that's neat. I went there once," he said, "when I was a little boy." It was shortly after his parents had married. The thought always brought a smile to Noel's lips. How many couples include a young boy on their honeymoon? But that's how it had always been for Noel and Jennifer, the woman his father had married. He considered Jennifer his mother in every sense of the word; she had included Noel in everything. He doubted a woman could love a child of her own body as much as Jennifer loved him, and he loved her. The three of them—Noel, his father, and his stepmother, Jennifer—had a very special relationship. Probably his parents' faith in God had a lot to do with it, he admitted to himself. "I don't remember too much about Greece," he continued. "Just that I liked it. How long have you lived here?"

"More than six years."

"Alone?"

ॐ

Natalia wasn't sure she liked that question. She didn't know much about this man, and she had made it her way never to be too open with anyone. People had preconceived notions about models—some of them arrived at correctly. But not where she was concerned. He didn't know she was a model—at least she didn't think he knew—but that possibility existed. So this was getting too personal for her. In case he did know—had, in fact, seen her picture and was using their "chance" meetings as an excuse to talk to her, though she didn't believe it—she wasn't going to give too much information away.

"Of course not." It wasn't a lie. She lived with Prince.

"Oh." She could tell from the way his face clouded over that he assumed she meant with a man. His disappointment was palpable. "You're married?"

"No."

"Oh," he said. She groaned inside. That "oh" meant he thought she lived with a man without being married. She couldn't let him think that, especially since he knew she was a Christian. "So you're in a relationship right now?"

She prayed that her thoughts about his being a decent person were true. "No. I don't live with a man. I would never live with a man who wasn't my husband. But I wasn't lying—I try never to do that either," she said, flashing a quick smile to relieve the self-righteous way it could be construed. "I live with Prince." She ruffled the dog's fur. "And I live in the same apartment building with my surrogate family here in New York."

The relief that crossed his face almost made her laugh and definitely made her thankful she'd been honest with him. "I'm glad," he admitted on a frosted breath that made his words seem to dance in delight around his head. She wasn't sure if he was glad because she didn't live with a man or because she hadn't altered his idea of how a Christian should behave. "It might sound funny in this day and age," he continued, "but it's nice to find a woman with old-fashioned values."

He was glad because of my second thought! That made her feel tingly down to her toes. But she wanted to clarify from where her standards originated. "I don't think my principles are really old-fashioned as much as God-fashioned." She lifted her brows and tilted her head toward him.

He nodded thoughtfully, something in itself that astounded her. Often such declarations on her part had been scoffed at. "Like my parents," he said.

She let out the breath she hadn't realized she'd been holding. "I think I'd like your parents," she admitted.

He chuckled. "I *know* they would like you."

The music, the sounds of happy shoppers on the street, taxis and buses and trucks passing them, faded as they looked deeply into one another's eyes, into one another's souls. What Natalia saw in the blueness of the man's eyes made her heart rejoice. That something very special was happening between them, an emotion deeper than time, was obvious. Natalia only prayed it was something God ordained. Somehow she felt that it was.

Tearing her gaze away from his, wanting to lighten a moment that was becoming too heavy, she turned toward the front of the line. She was relieved to see they were almost at the first window. She pointed to his camera. "You'd better get it ready." She glanced behind them. About a hundred people were there now. "With so many people wanting to see the windows, we can't stop for long."

She was relieved when, taking her cue to lighten the mood, he reached for his camera. She liked him and wanted to get to know him, but the emotions swirling within her needed to be tempered with time.

After a half hour of gazing together at the artistically re-created rooms in the store windows, all from the Victorian age and decorated for Christmas with garlands and tinsel, wreaths and ribbons, and greenery of every kind, Natalia glanced at her watch. "I really must go."

"Too bad. I was going to ask you to go to a little café and get a hot chocolate or something."

She gave a slight shiver, and for the first time since he had walked up to her side, she felt the cold. She fixed her scarf closer around her neck. "Perfect evening for it. I would have loved to. Maybe another time," she suggested.

"Definitely. But"—amusement glinted in his dark eyes— "if we're going to meet each other again, maybe we should exchange names."

She laughed. "For a person who loves onomastics I'm surprised that wasn't your first question."

"It normally is," he answered, his lips turning downward. "But with us nothing seems normal." The way he looked at her—with the gleam of a man who considers a woman special—made her forget about the cold again. "I like that."

"Me too," she heard herself whisper back.

She probably would have stood there gazing into his face for the next hour if he hadn't suddenly put out his hand and said, "Hi! I'm Noel Sheffield."

She extended her gloved hand to his waiting one. "Nice to meet you, Noel." She paused, then decided quickly to give him her real name, something she rarely did. "Natalia Pappas."

He whistled in appreciation of it. "Now that's some name. To be called Natalia, meaning 'of or relating to Christmas,' you must have been born around Christmas. And Pappas—well, you could most definitely be nothing other than Greek." His brows came together in a thoughtful question. "Isn't *pappas* what priests are called in Greek? I suppose there must be a long line of priests in your family."

"Very good." She was impressed. "And yes on both accounts. As a matter of fact, my father is a Greek Orthodox priest, as was his father, and his father before, and, well, I guess all the way back to the beginning of Christianity."

He whistled. "That's some lineage."

"It is kind of neat to know I was raised in a tradition that goes back almost two thousand years, practically to the Twelve Apostles and Christ, Himself. But—" She dipped her head and clamped her mouth shut. She could sometimes go on too much about history and her beliefs about things. She didn't want to do that with this man and risk alienating him from her.

"No, please continue," he encouraged her as he had at the tree the other day.

"Are you sure?" She grimaced slightly. "Once I start talking I don't seem to stop, and I have very strong beliefs and—"

"I want to hear them, Natalia," he whispered. "All of them."

All? She saw in his eyes an interest that went beyond the superficial. It was a heady feeling. Her father had always wanted to know everything her mother was thinking; anything important to her was important to him. Could this man feel the same way? And if he did, what did that say? That he cherished her? Cherished her thoughts? She still hesitated.

"Please go on." His eyebrows rose slightly, and he gave a quick, reassuring nod.

What else could I ask for? she thought. Taking a deep breath, she plunged in. "Well, the most important thing is that my father—my mother too when she was alive—has always made God the center of his life. Consequently God has always been the heart of our family's lives."

"I think that's as important to you as it is to my parents," he commented.

"It's the most important thing," she admitted and hoped he understood what she was trying to say. For them to have a future together, something she wished might be theirs, it would have to be the same for him. She hoped he understood that.

His right hand reached out toward her. When it settled on her left shoulder, heat enveloped her, and the noise, the bustle of the evening, seemed to slip away. It was as if they were the only two people on the avenue again as he smiled a crooked little smile down at her and said, "Well, we must meet for that cocoa sometime." He spoke softly with a husky, romantic sound to his voice that made her feel like the most valued woman alive. "Because I find I want to hear all about your beliefs, Natalia Pappas."

He looked away and squinted toward the bright lights. From the way his jaw clenched and unclenched, it seemed to Natalia as if he were considering something of importance.

"You might find it strange, but where I have never wanted to sit down and listen to my parents talk about their beliefs"—he looked back at her—"I want to with you. Very much."

She reached up and wrapped her gloved fingers around his. "It's not at all odd, Noel. How many children honestly ever want to pay attention to their parents?"

❧

As a counselor Noel knew that was true, but also as a counselor he felt convicted by her words. Was he ignoring the best advice his parents had to give? Since meeting this woman, he was beginning to think he was being as ornery as some of his high school students, even Rachel, whom he was so concerned about these days.

"Well, Noel." She let go of his hand and lowered hers to the dog's lead. The emptiness he felt over not holding it any longer was keen until she spoke her next words. "How about if we meet at the grandstand of the Thanksgiving Day parade? At seven in the morning. Perhaps we can go for cocoa afterward." She shivered slightly. "I heard the weather report last night, and it's supposed to keep getting colder and colder until Christmas. I think we'll have to thaw out after sitting outside for so long. I have tickets for the stands outside of Macy's, so we can enjoy the show up close."

"How do you have tickets?" he blurted out, then smiled sheepishly. "Sorry," he apologized. He knew grandstand tickets were hard to come by and much coveted. If he hadn't already realized there was something special about this woman, having grandstand tickets was one more indication.

"My surrogate parents, whom I mentioned earlier, receive them each year. But they won't be using them this year, so they've offered them to me." She patted Prince's head. "I was going to bring Prince as my date, but if you'd like to come. . . ?"

"As your date?"

If his tree at the center sparkled half as much as her eyes did right now—like soft blue diamonds reflecting the many-colored lights on the avenue—then he knew it would be the most beautiful tree ever. "As a friend," she said with a smile that made her lips crinkle at their corners in such a cute way he wished he could touch them.

To be a friend was good. He would take that. For now. "I'd like that."

She nodded. "Me too."

four

It was fantastic to see the Macy's Thanksgiving Day parade arrive at Herald Square with its world-renowned performers, the huge balloons fashioned in whimsical characters, the marching bands, the clowns, the magical floats. But to Noel the best part of the morning was being with the girl and her dog and going for hot chocolate afterward to a little café off Broadway. The arctic bite in the air had combined with the wind to give them both rosy cheeks. The warmth of the café was a welcome change from the outdoor elements.

Soft Christmas music filled the café, continuing the sounds heard on the city streets. Ginger and cinnamon and sugary delights mixed with the scent of pine to please their sense of smell, as much as the parade had that of their hearing and sight. Evergreen and wood, windowpanes frosted naturally by the elements outside, and a stone fireplace running the full length of an inside wall with a tall Christmas tree to its side helped make the café cozy and festive. Each little marble-topped table came complete with its own miniature tree decorated with lights that softly winked and blinked too.

Noel and Natalia found a table near the fireplace. They laughed over some of the antics of the people trying to keep the huge helium balloons from taking off in the high winds.

"I thought one of the young girls holding the tin soldier was going to lift off just as Santa's sled was mounted to do!"

Noel exclaimed. He mimicked the shock on the girl's face as her feet rose an inch off the ground, and they laughed until tears glistened in their eyes.

"Ah, Santa!" Natalia sighed as she wiped the corners of her eyes with her red holiday napkin. "Of course, the Santa Claus float is the best of all. His arrival into Herald Square officially opens the Christmas season in New York City and America."

That statement brought a quizzical frown to Noel's face. "You don't mind children believing in Santa Claus?" he asked, not waiting for a reply. He wanted to explain his question. "As Christians, my parents seem to be in a quandary about that. I was allowed to believe in him, though, when I was a young child." At the time his father hadn't seen any harm in letting Noel believe in Santa. But his father's views had changed through the years.

"That's a tough question," she replied. He watched her take a sip of her cocoa. "The Santa myth is such a delightful one for children to experience, especially here in America. It's become an American tradition, and I think Christians have to bear that in mind. But like many things surrounding the celebration of Christmas"—she pointed to the lights, the trees, the tinsel all around the room—"if we remember the reason behind it, then I think it's fine."

"Meaning?"

She shrugged. "Well, first of all, I think parents have to teach their children that Santa Claus was actually a man. He was a bishop in the church, and his name was Nicholas. He lived in Myra in Asia Minor and did much good, all in the name of the One he believed in and served his entire life—Jesus Christ. Even after Nicholas died, people remembered his life as an example of a wonderful Christian."

"You're talking about the man referred to as *Saint* Nicholas, right?"

She nodded. "Saint Nicholas of Myra. That's the one!"

"Okay, but what about children believing he lives forever?"

"Well. . ." She let the word roll off her lips in a hesitant way. "The truth is, as a Christian he *does* live forever. Bishop Nicholas was purported to have died on December 6, around the year A.D. 330. That day is celebrated as the first day of his life with Christ in paradise. In that manner, through his faith in Jesus, Nicholas of Myra, like all Christians, does indeed live on."

Noel knew his mouth dropped open at her words, but he couldn't have kept it from happening. She was saying things he had never heard before. "How do you know all this?"

She seemed to understand finally how much he enjoyed hearing her share her views, for excitement shone on her face, enchanting Noel with her eagerness. "Well, remember that my father is a priest—in the same tradition in which Nicholas of Myra was first a priest, then a bishop. Back in those days, Myra, the city in Asia Minor where Nicholas served as bishop, was a major part of the Greek world." She glanced toward the tree's lights and squinted in a way that almost seemed sad to him. "Until a few decades ago the city of Myra was Hellenic with mostly Greek Christians living there, even though the Turks from Asia had taken over the land politically during the Middle Ages."

Once again he realized there was more to her than outer beauty. Behind that golden hair, the blue eyes, and the features that looked like a master craftsman had sculpted them were brains. And she was knowledgeable about different things, things he had no idea about. As one who studied the etymology of names, he liked that. "I had no idea about any of this."

She sipped her cocoa, then said, "That's one of the nice things about cultures mixing with one another." She looked at him above the rim of her cup before replacing it on the table. "I'd never heard of some of the more current men and women of faith from this area of the world until coming to live here." She held up her hand and counted off a few people on her fingers. "D. L. Moody, Peter Marshall, and Billy Graham, for example. Those men and their walks through life should be remembered as much as the early Christians."

"I agree that history is very important. Does Myra still exist? I mean, are there still ruins from the time of Nicholas?"

"Oh, sure," she said, nodding. "Ancient Greek, Christian, and medieval Greek ruins are all over what is now modern Turkey. In Myra, the actual church where Nicholas taught, which was built during his lifetime, is still there. My father visited it when he was a young man. In fact, the church in our village is very similar in appearance."

"Wait a minute." Noel leaned forward. "He visited the exact church where Saint Nicholas preached?"

She nodded.

He whistled. "I never knew there was so much to the man who inspired the legend of Santa Claus."

"Not too many people in this part of the world seem to know much about the early Christians, Saint Nicholas included. I've noticed since moving here that everyone knows about the apostles, and then there seems to be a break until about the time of Martin Luther. But we grew up learning about early Christians in Kastro, the village I come from. Rather than having our rock stars or football stars, we have those men and women who gave their lives so today we could have the same knowledge they had about Christ. Saint Nicholas, the real man, has always been one of the more important Christians to remember. Even today."

Noel shook his head. "So Santa actually was real?"

"Definitely," she said without hesitation. "And because he was a Christian, he still lives. So that's true too. A Christian's body might die but not the spirit. So to say Santa still lives is true in the same way that all Christians live even when our bodies die." She returned to her original thought. "When a person knows Santa Claus was actually a wealthy young man who became a priest in the church and gave in Jesus' name so generously his deeds were talked about for generations, then it's fine to enjoy that tradition. But a person should not believe in him, rather in the One whom Saint Nicholas believed in and followed—Jesus Christ. Otherwise I think a child is in for a great disappointment on learning Santa doesn't live at the North Pole or fly through the sky on a sled pulled by reindeer."

Noel heaved a deep sigh. "To be honest, that realization was one of the hardest for me to accept." He had learned it at about the same time his mother died, when he was six. The two losses coming together were— Another thought, an aggressive, almost angry one, intruded upon the first. For the first time Noel understood he was angry at God about both events: His mother had died, and as crazy as it sounded for a man nearly twenty-eight, Santa had died too.

Worse.

Santa, as such, had never really lived.

It was a startling thing for Noel to realize.

Maybe it was one of the reasons he never wanted to

believe a baby born in a stable could be the God of the universe. If Santa was just a myth, then wasn't the idea of a baby born as fully God and fully Man also a myth?

But he knew enough to know there was a fallacy in his thinking.

There was a big difference between the two examples.

But not to a six-year-old child who had just lost his mother. To a grieving child it would be the same thing.

Worse even. For the baby who was God should have been able to save his mother for him. Noel remembered asking both Santa and Jesus to save her that year.

Neither had.

But he didn't want to get into this with Natalia now, so he kept the conversation on Santa Claus. "And I guess his name must have been derived somehow from the actual Nicholas."

"That's right. With your knowledge of names, can you figure it out?" she asked just before taking another sip of hot chocolate.

"Well, Nicholas is an ancient Greek name which means 'victory of the people.'"

She nodded. "Even today we say *nikisa* for victory. But more important we are certain Nicholas was Greek, of Hellenic heritage, by his name."

Now she was speaking on a subject with which he was familiar. "Absolutely. Back then names were never given lightly. They always told something about the person. Particularly from where they hailed. So let's see." He felt that thrill he always got when considering the history of names. It was like a tasty morsel to his mind. "How did his name go from being Nicholas, Greek bishop of Myra, to Santa Claus? There has to be an interesting etymology here."

"Want me to tell you?" She leaned forward and asked with all the eagerness of a child wanting to tell a secret.

He smiled and, sitting back, indicated with his hands to go ahead. He loved watching her talk, the way her mouth curved around each word as if it were a treasure and the way her eyes opened wide with an excitement similar to reading a good book.

"Well, the Dutch settlers of New Amsterdam"—she pointed out the window to the city by which it was first known to colonists—"brought with them their beloved *San Nicolaas*. Americans said it fast with a stress on the broad double *a* of the last syllable. A *t* slipped in after the first *n*, and we get *Santy Claus*. From there it was just a short step to Santa Claus. That's how American kids started calling the early Christian cleric from the Greek world Santa Claus!"

Noel shook his head in appreciation. "That's one of the more remarkable etymologies I've heard. But," he conceded, "it sounds correct."

"You're the expert in names, of course, but I think it is," she said with a bright smile. "Now enough about Santa." She glanced at her watch. "I have to get going soon or I'll miss Thanksgiving dinner. But how about telling me what you do?" She laughed. "We still seem to talk about everything but the normal things."

They hadn't had even one moment of boring "small talk" between them. "It's nice," he said. It was one of the things he liked about her.

She nodded and glanced at her watch again. "I agree, but if I'm going to tell my surrogate family about you at Thanksgiving dinner in about an hour, I should at least be able to tell them what you do."

He was pleased she was going to tell the people she was close to about him. It meant she must be beginning to care for him. Maybe even in more than just a friendly way.

He liked that. A lot.

"Okay." He sat up straight and wondered what he should tell her. He had told her about onomastics as a hobby. What he hadn't told her was that he was a writer and his current book was a huge success on the *New York Times* best-seller list.

He decided against enlightening her about it, though.

People always seemed to change toward him once they learned he was an author—particularly a successful one. He doubted she would, but he didn't want to take that chance. He didn't want her to act any differently than she had been. "I come from a very long line of lawyers, one that stretches back to revolutionary days."

"That's quite a lineage," she said, repeating his earlier words about her and her priestly ancestry.

"By American standards, it is. But I guess it kind of pales when compared to Greek ones."

She shook her head. "No. Don't say that. Everything is relative. America is new."

"Tell me something?" He leaned forward. "How old is the church in your village?"

Her gaze searched the ceiling, as though she might discover the answer there. "I don't know. It's from Byzantine times, so it must be at least five or six hundred years old, maybe older."

He held up his hands and smiled. "I rest my case."

She laughed. "You spoke just like a lawyer. Are you one too?"

"Only by degree."

Her brows came together. "What do you mean?"

"I studied criminal law, even graduated from Harvard Law School, but I'm a high school counselor." He shrugged his shoulders. This was what most women couldn't understand. Why he would be a high school counselor when he could be a high-powered, highly paid criminal lawyer with one of the oldest firms in the city. But she didn't know about his wealth—that he never had to work a day in his life if he didn't want to—and, for the moment, he would keep it that way.

He was shocked when he saw a look of wonder in her eyes. Just the opposite of what he normally saw in a woman's face when he told of his career choice. "Really. Well, a counselor is a counselor whether it is to direct people in the ways of the law or children in the way of life. I think, of the two, you chose the better."

He was taken aback. "You do?"

"Of course. You have the chance to shape young minds so that maybe they won't need the help of your other profession when they grow older."

She couldn't have shocked him more had she said she was going to walk across the Brooklyn Bridge. "That is exactly my reasoning. Precisely why I decided to counsel high school-age people."

"I know someone else who did something similar. Stavros Andreas is my village's schoolteacher. Because the village doesn't have too many children, he teaches all ages. But he left a career as a university professor here in the States—at Georgetown University, I think—and went to live in his ancestral village. That is my village of Kastro, and he did it so he could raise his daughter himself and, as he has often said, 'to help form young minds.' He has never regretted his decision. Especially since

Allie Alexander, the village doctor, left New York and came to the village, and they fell in love—"

Noel held up his hand. "Wait a minute. Is this the fairy-tale romance between the teacher and the doctor you mentioned at the center the other day?"

Her face brightened more. "That's it!"

"They sound like interesting people."

Her smile deepened. "They are. Stavros's faith had been, well—let's just say he had been really hurt by his first wife—"

"He's divorced?"

"No. His wife died. But they had been separated. She had hurt him terribly. His wife hadn't wanted their little daughter, Jeannie." Natalia shrugged her shoulders. "From what I understand, the woman never wanted to be a mother. She was a lawyer who wanted a career, and she deserted both her little girl and her husband."

"That's tough."

"But it's another case of God taking something terrible and making something wonderful. Allie, Stavros, and their four children couldn't be happier. Stavros regained his faith and was given the family he had always yearned for as well." She looked down at Prince who was sleeping by their feet under the table. "Prince is from their dog's litter of puppies."

"Really?" He glanced down at the dog. Who would have thought such a handsome German shepherd would come from a Greek village? Leaning forward, he reached for Natalia's hand. It was warm and soft, so soft he felt as if he were holding a cotton puff. "Now. I've told you about me, and you've told me about Allie and Stavros, and even Prince." He smiled down at the dog. "How about telling me about what you do so I can tell my parents when they ask me about any special people in my life?"

When the pupils of her eyes seemed to expand and swallow up some of the crystal blue of her irises, he was afraid he had gone a bit too far in describing how he felt about her. But as her lips softly curved up at their corners, he knew she didn't mind. Maybe she even liked it.

"Well, I—" She paused, and he thought she was trying to decide what exactly she should tell him. He understood. She had to be careful. They had met several times now, but they didn't know anyone in common. And this was New York City. "I'm a fashion-design student at Fashion Institute of Technology."

"No kidding?" That meant she was an artist. "You mean you're one of those people who can sketch clothes super quick."

She laughed. "Believe me, Noel—sometimes I don't think quickly enough."

"I can't seem to draw a straight line, so people who can draw anything at all really impress me."

"I've always liked it a lot."

"How much longer do you have until you graduate?" Now that she was talking about herself, he was going to ask as much as he could.

"Next term."

"Fantastic. And then?"

She took a deep breath. "Then I hope to start my own line of clothes."

"And you have been going to school for six years?" That's how long she'd told him she'd been in New York. But he knew she must have been doing something more than just going to school. She had to support herself. New York was an expensive place to live. And he already knew what her father did.

"Yes, but part-time. I've been working too."

"Doing what?"

"A bit of modeling," she murmured.

That surprised him. Not that she was a model. She certainly could be. Just that he didn't expect a strong Christian to be in that industry. "What type of modeling do you do, if you don't mind my asking?"

"No, of course not." She tucked a long strand of hair behind her ear, and he had the impression this line of questioning had made her uncomfortable. Giving her the benefit of his own experience, he suspected it was for the same reason he didn't like telling people he was a writer. People treated him differently.

She flashed a self-conscious smile before continuing. "For some reason I'm often asked to model nurses' uniforms."

"Nurses' uniforms?" He had the feeling she had modeled more than nurses' uniforms, but he didn't push her.

Her mouth turned up in an amused way. "Tell me—do you think I look like a nurse?"

She was giving him the chance to look at her, really look at her, and it wasn't an opportunity he was going to pass up.

From her soft forehead to her full lips, he let his gaze roam over her face. Did she look like a nurse? He wasn't so sure about a nurse, but he thought the look of gentleness and wisdom in her eyes, plus her height, which must be close to five feet ten inches, probably got her jobs modeling the white nurses' uniforms. An aura of purity seemed to surround her like perfume. Other than being gorgeous to see, she had a look of capability about her. Yes, he could imagine her dressed as a nurse.

"Hey!" she exclaimed after a moment, reaching for Prince's lead. He knew he'd taken too much time and had made her feel uncomfortable.

He quickly leaned forward. "No, wait." He touched her hand. "Yes. I can see where you might make the perfect nurse. You give a feeling of competency."

She loosened her grip on the lead. "Thanks. That's a nice thing to say." She glanced at her watch. "But I have to go—"

"Me too." He had to catch the train out to New Jersey in fifteen minutes; otherwise, he would be late for Thanksgiving dinner at his parents'. And he didn't want to do that. "But look. Since we both love Christmas activities, how about if you and Prince, if you like, come with me to the tree-lighting ceremony at Rockefeller Center in three days? I have passes for the guest section."

Her pale brows rose. "The guest section? How?"

"I have a connection with the tree."

"With—the—tree?" she questioned in staccato.

"Don't worry. I'm not into any mysticism connected with trees. I have the passes because my parents donated the tree this year. It comes from their property in New Jersey."

He had the satisfaction of seeing her eyes widen. "It did?" But immediately they narrowed. "Oh, how could they part with it? That is the only thing about the trees at the center that has bothered me. They are cut down."

"No, it's okay," he assured her. "This tree has been marked for Rockefeller Plaza since, well, ever since my father was a little boy. Norway spruces have a life span of only 80 to 110 years. My great-grandfather planted this tree over 100 years ago. It wouldn't have been able to survive many more hard winters. Either that or it would have soon died of old age."

"I didn't realize their life span was that short. So your family wanted it to have a chance to show its beauty to the world?"

"That's right," Noel agreed and was glad she understood. "Please come with me to see it lit, Natalia. It would mean a great deal to me to have the woman by my side who loves and appreciates the center's trees so much she comes to welcome them upon their arrival every year." It would mean that and so much more. He wanted her to attend the special ceremony with him more than he could ever remember wanting anything in recent years.

Her lips curved up into that giving smile he was coming to expect from her. As her fingers squeezed his gently, Noel wondered at the way she made him feel, as if he wanted to hold her, protect her, never let her out of his sight. She was the mate of his soul, the woman his eyes yearned to see every day, forever. "I would be honored, Noel."

His heart seemed to bang louder inside his chest. A date. A real date. One that might end with his placing his lips on hers. "May I pick you up at your home?" he pushed out past his throat that had suddenly gone dry.

At first her eyes flashed with pleasure over the idea, but when they dulled and she shook her head, disappointment sliced through him. "No. Not at my home, but at my surrogate parents' home." She reached into her purse for a pen and, leaning over, wrote something on a napkin. "This is their address. I would like for you to meet them before we go out."

"On our *date?*" he asked, placing special emphasis on the word as he slipped the napkin into his pocket. He had to make sure she saw it that way too. It would change their relationship. He wanted it. But did she?

She flashed that million-dollar smile of hers, one that made her whole face shine like the sun. "Yes, on our date," she agreed, and Noel felt sure his smile had to be a reflection of hers.

Finally he would have a date with Natalia, a real one. Not just an outing as friends. As he paid and they walked out of the café together, it took every ounce of his self-control not to skip down the sidewalk.

five

It took a lot to impress Noel. But the apartment building did just that when a uniformed doorman let him inside on the afternoon of the day his tree was to be lit. He knew the pre-war building was one of the great luxury apartment buildings in Manhattan. He rode the gilt elevator to the top floor.

"Welcome and come in," a woman greeted him, smiling warmly. She ushered him into the entrance hall. It had stone detailing on the walls and marble on the floors, reminding him of châteaus he had visited while in France. "You must be Noel. I'm Janet Howard, Natalia's, well—" She gave a light laugh that was full of good cheer. "I call myself her surrogate mother."

Noel shook Janet Howard's hand. "I've heard her refer to you in that way."

"My husband and I have been blessed with three sons." She guided him into the living room where the soothing strains of Christmas carols played softly in the background. "We are happy to count Natalia as a daughter. But please come in and sit down. Both my husband and Natalia will be out shortly," she said and motioned to a spacious room that made Noel feel more like he was in a Parisian apartment than one in Manhattan. Then he looked out the many windows at the panoramic view it had of Central Park and knew he could be nowhere but in his beloved New York City. The apartment sat just above tree level. The park was laid out below in its leafless, wintertime splendor.

"That's beautiful," he said, motioning to the view before he sat on the velvet sofa behind him.

Janet stood for a moment more and looked out the window at the view. Noel thought she must have gazed upon it a thousand times before. To him, she seemed to be breathing it in as if for the very first time.

"My husband and I have lived here for the last forty years, and yet"—she shook her head at the wonder of it—"I never tire of looking out these windows. It's one of God's greater blessings in our lives." She sat in a chair adjacent to his. "I grew up on a farm in Connecticut," she explained. "To have trees within my view is almost a must for me." She turned and smiled at the older woman who brought in a silver tray laden with tea and coffee, cakes and sandwiches. "May I offer you something?" she asked with a gracious wave of her hand over the tray. "Juanita makes the best coffee in the world."

Noel leaned forward. That was of interest to him. He was a connoisseur of great coffee. He smiled at the older woman in the maid's uniform. "In that case I'd like a cup. And a piece of that chocolate confection too."

Though employer and employee, the two women were obviously friends, and they shared a laugh of mutual delight. "Just what we like, right, Juanita? A man who both appreciates and admits to wanting delicious food." Janet Howard waved the other woman aside as she started to serve. "I'll take care of it, Dear. Thank you."

Noel nodded at the maid as she smiled and left the room.

Janet glanced up at the Charles X clock on the mantel. "Her favorite show is coming on TV," she whispered to him. "I hate for her to miss it," she said, pouring the coffee. "Cream? Sugar?"

"No. Black is fine."

Janet nodded and handed it to him, then sliced the silver knife through the luscious-looking cake. "Are you planning to go out anywhere after the tree-lighting ceremony?"

Noel looked at her in surprise. It had been years since a date's parents, or even parent-type figures, had asked him what his plans were for the evening.

Janet returned his gaze with a steady one, and he realized she was serious. She passed him a plate with a slice of cake. Where Natalia was concerned, he could understand the older woman's care and appreciate it. "I've made reservations at the Tavern on the Green for afterward." He referred to the famous restaurant located in Central Park.

"Oh! That's one of Natalia's favorite places, especially at this time of the year. It's decorated for Christmas. It has become our tradition to take her there for her birthday each year." She looked up, startled. "Oh, that's next week! I must remember to make reservations."

Noel paused in putting a forkful of cake in his mouth. "Her birthday is next week?" His own birthday was too. He wondered if it might fall on the same date.

"The first day of Advent. December the first. That's why she's named—"

"Natalia," Noel finished for her, and his eyes widened. They shared the same birthday.

Janet looked at him in surprise. "Why, yes."

"That's why I'm called Noel," he explained. "My birthday is the first day of Advent too."

"Oh!" Janet clapped her hands together at the coincidence of it. When Natalia and an older, distinguished-looking gentleman walked into the room arm in arm, she turned to them. "Natalia, you and Noel share the same birthday!"

Natalia's blue gaze met his. To Noel, as he stood up, it was as if the other two people weren't there. She had been beautiful the other times he had seen her, but now, dressed specifically for him and for their first real date, she looked like a modern-day, fairy princess should. She wore a burgundy cowl-neck sweater with a matching knee-length velvet skirt and high black boots that had ankle straps with antique brass buckles on them. But it was the look in her eyes that made all the finery fade almost beyond consequence. Her eyes shone like diamonds reflecting the light, and Noel had to remind himself to breathe.

"*Your* birthday is December the first?" There was that quality in her voice of a young girl pleased by the discovery.

He could only nod.

She moved forward. Actually she seemed to float toward him.

She extended her slim hands to him, her expression softening.

"Oh, Noel." She paused as the thought occurred to her. "*That's* why you're called 'Noel'?"

He nodded. "It means 'Christmas.' " The meaning behind his own name was one of the reasons he had started studying onomastics.

"And yours means the same," Janet Howard said. "How remarkable."

"Something else we have in common," he whispered to Natalia, and she nodded her golden head slightly before turning to the man who was standing behind her. "Jasper Howard, I'd like for you to meet Noel Sheffield." Extending the same honor to Noel she said, "Noel, Jasper Howard."

"It's good to meet you, Sir," Noel replied and shook hands.

"Sheffield?" The older man looked at him with the narrowed gaze of a man trying to place another. "Is your father Quincy Sheffield of Sheffield, Brokaw, and Thomas?"

Noel saw in the man's eyes that light of interest he was used to seeing when someone recognized his prestigious family. He stiffened but nodded. He didn't like having to be associated with his family's law firm in order to see that look in another's eye. He was actually disappointed to see it in this man whom Natalia thought of so highly. But since it had happened all his life he was used to it and answered truthfully. "Yes, Sir."

"But Natalia told us you don't work in your father's firm?"

"No, Sir, I don't. If I did, though, I would work with my father, who does mostly pro bono cases."

"Yes, I've heard that. Your father is a Christian, isn't he?"

That surprised Noel more than anything else the man could have asked. No one, with the exception of Natalia, had asked him that before. Noel stood a bit straighter as he answered, taking sudden pleasure from doing so. "Yes, he is."

Jasper shook his head and smiled. "I've heard many good things about your father. The world would be a much better place if there were more men like your father in positions of responsibility. You must be very proud to be the son of a man of such well-placed principles."

Noel hadn't realized how highly he esteemed his father until that moment. "Yes, I'm proud of both my father and my mother."

Noel saw Natalia flash a see-I-told-you-so smile at her surrogate parents before saying, "We must be going." While she gathered her coat and scarf, Noel realized he didn't feel the need to make a hasty retreat from these people as he had when he was a young adult wanting to get away from a girl's relatives. It was a strange but good feeling.

"It was nice to meet you both," Noel said and shook hands again with Jasper. To Janet he said, "Please tell Juanita her cake and coffee were delicious."

"Juanita must take credit for the coffee, but the cake was my creation."

Noel's brows lifted in surprise. Most women he knew who had full-time help didn't do much in the kitchen. "It was fantastic."

Jasper Howard put his arm around his wife's waist. "Everything my wife does is fantastic," he said in a loving, yet not boastful, way. Noel could feel the air around them radiating with the love they felt for one another, exactly as it did around his own parents. It was something wonderful and perfect and special. He only wished, as he helped Natalia on with her coat—a gray, double-faced, cashmere design that was soft to the touch—that he and this woman whose birthday he shared might find such a love someday.

The older couple walked with them to the door. "It must be very special to see *your* tree being lit," Janet Howard commented.

Noel looked over at Natalia. The boots she wore almost made her his height. "It's even more so by having Natalia with me," he admitted and looked back in time to catch Janet and Jasper Howard exchanging amused glances.

"Have a wonderful evening, you two," Jasper said while Natalia reached over and planted a quick kiss on first his cheek then Janet's.

"We will."

As they stepped out the door, Noel stopped suddenly. "Hey! Haven't you forgotten someone?"

The three looked at him in confusion.

"Where's Prince?"

Their faces settled into smiles, and Natalia slipped her left arm through his right one. Noel couldn't remember the last time anything had felt better. "I thought I would hold onto you tonight."

Noel looked over at her surrogate family and gave them a small wink. "I like the way that sounds."

ə

The tree-lighting ceremony was everything and more than Noel had thought it would be. The only thing that would have made it better would have been to have had his parents with them. They had planned on coming into the city for the occasion, but his mother had developed a cold. Having suffered from pneumonia the previous winter, they deemed it prudent to stay at home and watch the ceremony on TV.

Noel missed them but was glad he had Natalia with whom to enjoy it. When the giant TV screen at the center showed his tree being trussed, then cut down on his parents' property, Noel thought it had to be the most novel way to introduce a girl to his parents' affluent home.

When the Tudor-style mansion was shown, Natalia leaned toward him and whispered, "Your mother has made a model of *that* house?"

He nodded but braced himself for what would most likely follow—her understanding of his parents' wealth.

"Must be a beautiful dollhouse."

Noel turned to her. She was actually thinking about the difficulty in re-creating the mansion as a dollhouse rather than about what the historic home represented—generations of wealth.

That was a first for him.

By this time he would usually see dollar signs in the eyes of women. He saw none in Natalia's. They still sparkled like diamonds, but for the occasion and not for his wallet.

He quickly realized the fallacy of his jaded thinking. Her beliefs wouldn't allow her to be impressed by wealth except, like his parents, in the context of how it might help others. After seeing the Howards' luxury apartment, he should have known the stateliness of his parents' home wouldn't faze her. Her own apartment was located in the same building.

The show included famous singers performing Christmas songs, Olympic champion skaters, the Radio City Rockettes, and even someone dressed as Santa waving and dancing to a merry tune across the stage. Then the time for the lighting of the tree finally arrived.

"Noel." Natalia leaned over and spoke directly into his ear. With all the happy noises going on around them, that was the only way to be heard. Noel was glad; he liked the closeness, savored the way her perfume scented the air around them. "Do you know who is going to turn the switch that lights the tree this year?"

"I think the mayor will."

It was the mayor, and soon the countdown began. "Ten. Nine. Eight. Seven. Six. Five. Four. Three. Two. One!"

A gigantic shout erupted.

The switch was turned on.

Thousands of lights lit the tree. And everyone looked on it with childlike wonder, the multicolored lights illuminating each person.

"It's a fairyland of delight!" Natalia said among all the "oohs" and "aahs" and clapping around them.

Noel had to agree. It *was* like a fairyland: a beautiful land of wonder and enchantment, goodness and light. And *his* tree was at the center of it all.

"How do you feel?" Natalia asked into his ear.

He turned his head so their gazes met.

How *did* he feel? The word that came to him he had never used. But it was the only one that described what this moment meant to him. He leaned toward her and spoke it.

"Blessed," he said. Her eyes narrowed as if to ascertain she had heard correctly. He nodded and mouthed the word again. "Blessed."

She reached for his hand and patted it gently, and a feeling of blessedness that even he could recognize as coming from God increased within him. As everyone started singing "Joy to the World" and praising the One whom the tree was meant to glorify, Noel wondered how he had ever lived without the feeling singing through his soul. And how he had ever lived without this remarkable girl.

ॐ

"That was one of the most wonderful things I've ever experienced," Natalia said after the host at the Tavern on the Green seated them at their table. "The tree couldn't have looked better. And what a surprise this is." She looked around the restaurant. "I usually come here only for my birthday."

"So Janet told me. That's how we found out you and I share the same one."

"I know! Why don't you come with us this year?"

"That would be great, but I always spend it with my parents—"

"Of course you do. How silly of me!" She felt the heat of embarrassment fill her face.

"But that's in the evening," he was quick to point out, apparently trying to relieve her discomfiture. She appreciated it.

"How about if we make a *date?*" He paused as he accentuated the word.

Understanding he meant it in its true form, as a romantic appointment, she smiled.

"Let's make a date," he repeated, "to come to the park first thing in the morning of December 1. To be here"—he waved his hand over a small section of the huge park—"before anybody else. That would be a fun way to celebrate our birthdays. And with this freezing weather we might even have snow that day."

She felt laughter bubble up inside her. This was one of the things she liked about Noel. He did different things. No movie and a dinner date for him. They did unusual and special things. "I'd like that. I've never come out very early because of safety reasons."

"Well, I'll come to your apartment and get you. Between Prince, me, and"—he pointed upward—"your faith in God, you'll have nothing to fear."

She liked the fact that he had included God in the list, although she wasn't quite sure whether it was in a mocking way or not. When his next words came out, they not only settled the question in her mind, but thrilled her.

"I must admit, I'm beginning to envy you, my parents, and the Howards for your faith in God."

She reached for his hand and gave it a gentle squeeze. "It's not something you have to envy, Noel. It's something that can be yours so easily. It's about your volition, your choice, as a human being to believe or not to believe Jesus is who the Bible says He is."

"I believe He was a great man, Natalia, a great politician, a great moral teacher. Probably even the most important person in history to have ever lived," he conceded. "But God's Son?" He sighed, and she heard the regret in his tone. "That I don't get."

Natalia felt her heart beat fast with the desire to hand this special man her faith. But she knew it didn't work that way. It went back to volition, that gift of choice from God that made humans. . .well. . .human. To decide whether Jesus was who He said He was, was something people had to choose for themselves.

But Noel was questioning now, probably things his parents had been praying he would for many years. Saying a quick prayer, she reached for the crystal goblet of water and took a sip before speaking. She knew she could speak her mind because Noel had encouraged her often enough to do so. "Noel, do you know that on many occasions Jesus declared Himself to be God?"

"God's Son," he corrected her.

"Yes, He said He was God's Son—one Person of the Trinity—but also that He's God."

His brows came together in a frown. "Where did He say that?"

She breathed out deeply and said a prayer that her father's teachings might come back to her. "Well, in the Book of John it's recorded that He said, ' "I and the Father are one." ' "

"So what does that mean? To my way of thinking, it means He's God's Son—'I *and* the Father'—not God."

"Actually it means both. With those few words He's telling us He is both God's Son and God. Listen: ' "I and the Father are one." ' My own father"—she touched her chest as she referred to her *baba*—"once gave a lesson on the fact that the term 'one' in Greek is neuter, meaning 'one thing,' not 'one person.' In other words the two—Jesus the Son of God and God the Father—are one in essence or nature, but They are not identical Persons."

He frowned. "So how many Gods are there?"

"One."

"But you just said"—he paused as he seemed to listen in his mind to exactly what she had said—" ' "one thing," not "one person." ' "

"That's right. The verb 'are' used here indicates the Father and the Son are two Persons. Distinct, but united in essence, will, and action. God is one Entity but made up of three Persons—the Father, the Son, and the Holy Spirit."

"The Trinity?" he asked.

She nodded, relieved he knew the concept and she didn't have to explain where the three Persons suddenly seemed to come from.

"Okay, so Jesus is saying He is God here in this one place—"

"And He says it elsewhere."

"Where?"

Natalia drew in a deep breath and was grateful the waiter chose that moment to take their order. She was glad she'd told Noel to order for her—anything but liver—so she could get her thoughts together. She had relied so long on her father to guide people that it was a bit strange for her to be the one to do it now. Even with her years in New York, no one had ever asked her point-blank so many questions of such deep import. *Dear Lord,* she prayed silently, *please give me the words, the words my* baba *might use.*

And it was as if a voice answered her. *"Just think about what your baba has taught people—you included—throughout the years. You have heard it often enough. Just think. And My Holy Spirit will guide you. Only trust."*

The waiter left, and Noel sat back and looked at her. "You look pale. I'm sorry. I probably shouldn't have asked so many questions—"

"No." She held up her hand. She wouldn't let this opportunity pass. "Your asking me makes me very happy, Noel." She cupped her hands together on the edge of the table. "Believe me—it's like a gift. What would hurt is if you didn't want to know."

"I really do want to learn. It's strange. My parents have been trying to teach me things for years, but until now, until meeting you"—he held his hands out in a shrugging way—"I had little real interest. But you intrigue me. And the fact that you believe so strongly makes me want to know why. Does that make sense?"

Her heart seemed to pick up its tempo. "It makes perfect sense. I would want to know if the situation were reversed."

"You would?"

Emotion threatened to clog her throat. "You are becoming very special to me, Noel. But the fact that you don't know Jesus. . .would prove"—she had to swallow—"to be a stumbling block to our forming any lasting relationship. So your asking is hope—for me, for us—that we might"—she paused and, holding her hands together against her chin as if she were praying, ventured to finish with—"have a future together."

"Natalia," he whispered. Rather than her words scaring him away, as she feared they might, they seemed to have done just the opposite—draw them together. "I so badly want that with you. I have from—"

"Shh." She touched her finger to her lips. "Let's not say anything else yet. It's too soon."

He nodded, but she didn't think it was in agreement to its being too soon. "So you said there are other places where Jesus declared He's God, not just God's Son?" he asked.

She took a deep breath and let it out slowly. "If I had my Bible with me, I could show you."

"That's okay. Whatever you remember." He surprised her with his encouragement. But she shouldn't have been. Wasn't he always encouraging her to speak her thoughts, her beliefs? How could she do otherwise?

"Okay. Well, in the Gospel of John, the fourteenth chapter, Jesus said some of His most forceful words about His deity. In the sixth verse He said, ' "I am the way and the truth and the life. No one comes to the Father except through me." ' "

"I've heard that before. How does that prove His divinity?"

"Well, ' "the way and the truth and the life" ' is a Person. It's another name for Jesus."

"You mean those are all His names?"

She had forgotten about his love of onomastics. "That's right. Well, some of His names anyway," she clarified. "He has a lot of them." *Ask him to study My names.* The thought popped into her head. *Yes, Lord,* she answered. *Yes!* "Noel, you love to learn about names, right?"

"Yes," he answered slowly.

"Why?"

"Why what?"

"Why do you like to study names?"

"Because they're important. In older times a name identified a person. Among other things, like telling where a person came from—as we said the other day concerning Saint Nicholas—they were used to reflect personal experience or express or influence one's character."

"Exactly!" she exclaimed, but then she lowered her voice when she saw people from a nearby table glance in her direction. "And nowhere is that more true than in Bible times, both the Old and New Testaments." She opened her hands before her. "So why don't you study the Lord's names? Maybe you'll come to know who He is through learning about His names."

Noel sat back, and she could tell from the way his dark brows nearly touched that the thought intrigued him. "Hmm, might not be a bad idea." He leaned forward. "As a matter of fact, it's a good one."

"You know, I've heard of people—lawyers even—who started out to prove to the world that Jesus was a fraud only to fall at His feet in worship of His divinity. And all because of their studying about Him."

"Natalia," he said, his voice husky, "I would be very happy if the same thing happened to me."

"Me too, Noel." She blinked at the tears that had gathered in the corners of her eyes. *Dear God, please,* she implored. *Please give him Your understanding.*

"Do you remember any other places where Jesus says He's God?" he asked after a moment. Ducking her head down, she smiled. God seemed to be answering her prayer by Noel's persistence. He wanted to understand.

"Well, in the same chapter of John He said, ' "I am in the Father and the Father is in me." ' That means—"

"That He and the Father are one in essence and undivided."

She was impressed. Without a softened heart she thought it must be almost impossible for a person to grasp the concept even if that was precisely what it meant. "That's right."

He whistled softly. "That's quite a statement. Someone would either have to be a lunatic or, in truth, God to say such a thing."

"Precisely! That's why for you to say, as you did earlier, that you believe Jesus was a great man, a great politician, a great moral teacher, is an absurd declaration. On many occasions Jesus also declared Himself to be God."

A frown slashed across his face. "I see what you mean. The one crosses out the other, doesn't it?"

"How can a person be a great moral teacher if people don't believe all He said about Himself? Jesus said He was God. He said it so often the leaders and people of His day wanted to kill Him."

"And didn't they? Kill Him, I mean?"

"They didn't do anything to Him that He didn't allow, Noel." She lowered her voice. "When the time was right for Him, He allowed them to kill Him, after He had completed His ministry on earth. And with His resurrection He established His church, the rock upon which believers in Christ's redemptive work would flourish."

Noel repeated the words she had spoken a few minutes earlier: " ' "I am the way and the truth and the life. No one comes to the Father except through me." ' "

Natalia felt adrenaline flow through her body. To see Noel try to understand the Christian message was the most thrilling thing she had ever experienced. It was almost like watching a baby try to walk for the first time.

"That's right," she said. "And because of what Jesus did, if we choose to believe what He said about Himself—all His words, not just a select few—we will be resurrected as He was. We will be given brand-new bodies that will never perish, never get sick. And we will see loved ones who have gone on before us." From the way his gaze intensified and his blue eyes darkened to look like a midnight sky, she felt that was something very important to him. For the first time she wondered if perhaps he had lost someone close to him to death's sting. "Best of all, though," she continued, "we will be in complete fellowship with God for eternity."

She looked at the happy people around them and smiled. No one could say there wasn't something special about how people acted at this time of the year in America. In Greece it happened both at Christmas and at Easter time. "I like to think of this season, when goodwill seems to abound more than at any other time, as a glimpse of what heaven will be like, though it will be far more wonderful." Reaching over to the tree to her right, she detached a beautiful, handcrafted Christmas-tree ball from it. Moving the golden globe around in her hand so that all the colored lights from the room were reflected in its shiny glass, she said, "I think heaven will be so much more superior, though, like the sun in the sky is to this Christmas-tree ball."

"I wonder if that's why I've always liked this season most of all. Because it is a bit like everyone's idea of heaven."

She replaced the ornament and, taking his hand, lightly squeezed it. "It could be, Noel."

"Natalia, I *want* to believe. I really wish I could say, 'Okay, I believe you.' It's just that—"

"Shh," she said. "I understand."

"You do?"

She sat back and took a sip of water before answering. "People come to the Lord in different ways, Noel. It's possible your way will be through the study of His names. Even then I can't be sure." She replaced her glass and, resting her palms on the linen tablecloth, said, "But I feel it will happen."

"I *want* it to happen, Natalia. It's the only thing that has stood between my parents and me. I feel somehow it's true. I just have to know it is in here." He touched his heart.

She couldn't agree with his reasoning more. "That's the only way God wants a person, Noel. Many have the wrong idea about God. But, you know, I think one of the reasons God gave us the ability to read and study is to learn about Him. Perhaps it's laziness and the traditions of ancestry that keep people from opening the Bible and learning."

"Funny, but that's something I often tell my students."

She could understand laziness but not the other. "Tradition has to do with their not learning?"

"You'd be surprised how many kids think an education should come to them by osmosis. Or because their parents learned or didn't learn and they did okay, so the kids think they shouldn't have to study, either. So many waste the marvelous education they have available to them at the school in which I work."

Growing up in the village of Kastro, Natalia had never seen that. And the competition for entrance into her university had been so tough that most felt privileged to be there. "I suppose you're right." Then another thought came to her. "Noel, do you have a Bible?"

"Sure. I even have a study Bible with a concordance. My parents gave it to me a few Christmases ago." He shrugged his broad shoulders. "I haven't read more than the Christmas story." He twisted his head to the side. "Guess I should study it, huh?"

The waiter came then and placed their artistically designed plates of scrumptious-looking food before them.

"It's your choice, Noel," Natalia said. "Either it can stay dusty, or you can brush it off and use it, and"—she smiled brightly, trying to give him hope—"you can learn."

six

Later that night in his brownstone town house on the Upper West Side—ironically directly across the park from Natalia's apartment on the Upper East Side—Noel wondered about the things they had discussed. After searching his bookshelf, he found his Bible in a back corner. It was in such a forgotten location that not even his competent housekeeper's vacuuming had managed to keep the dust off its upper edge. Noel blew on it and coughed as the particles swirled around his head.

He opened the book. It seemed so foreign to him. Something his parents should be reading. Not him.

Walking over to his four-poster bed, he sat on the thick burgundy quilt. He was careful to move the ecru afghan his mother had made for him to the side. He'd told Natalia he would try to learn about Christ by studying His names. But how could he study Jesus' names when he didn't even know more than a couple?

He sighed. That was a cop-out. But he was too tired to reason it out. He put the Bible on his night table.

He would start tomorrow. Maybe.

❧

"I don't know, Prince," Natalia said to her dog about a half hour after Noel brought her back to her apartment. She sat on the thick white flocate, a rug from Greece made of sheep's wool, in front of the fireplace.

She glanced up at her dollhouse on the table to her side. Its windows were ablaze with the little electrical lights she had installed herself, and in honor of the season, wreaths hung on each door and a lighted tree stood in the bay window.

A gas fire burned in the apartment fireplace while Handel's *Messiah* played softly in the background. She was brushing the dog's shiny fur. It was a nightly winter ritual they both enjoyed. "I think Noel wants to learn, but the tradition of his not knowing and believing in his own brand of Christianity will be tough for him to break. And even though I suggested he start learning about Christ by studying His names, I doubt that's enough. I don't think he knows how to begin, Prince. I want to do more. But what?"

The dog turned his large head to her and nudged his nose against her hand. It was a comforting gesture he often gave her. Natalia put the brush down and, wrapping her arms around his back and chest, leaned her head against his clean fur and listened to the rhythmic *beat, beat, beat* of her beloved companion's heart. Steady and clear, it never failed to ease the worries of Natalia's own heart. "Dear Lord," Natalia prayed to her heavenly Father, "please show me what to do, how to help Noel."

The rest of their evening at the Tavern on the Green had progressed much the same, with him asking questions and her answering to the best of her ability. By the time dessert came they had moved on in conversation to talk about his work, and he had told her about the student, Rachel, with whom he was particularly concerned.

Natalia's heart reached out to the confused teenager. It amazed her how people went from being little kids to acting as grown-ups and dating so quickly in modern American culture. Teenagers here seemed in a big rush to become adults; it was not that way in Kastro. Natalia might be nearly ten years older than Noel's student, but she knew she was far younger in terms of the dating game, for which Natalia was very grateful.

Until Noel, no other man had truly interested Natalia as a possible life mate.

Growing up in Kastro, her friend Dimitri had hoped for more with her than the brotherly love she had always felt toward him, but even he had finally admitted to their not having that "special something" that should exist between a man and a woman. She was thankful he had finally turned to Maria, who had loved him all her life. From Martha's reports on the romance, Natalia was almost certain she would soon hear wedding bells pealing for Dimitri and Maria.

But Natalia knew everything was different with Noel. For the first time, she felt that "special something" for a man, and she knew Noel felt it for her too. If his beliefs could get into line with the precepts of Christianity Jesus had laid out, she would be very happy to spend her life with him.

As it was, she could hardly wait for their mutual birthday in three days' time. Their date for an early morning tryst at Central Park sounded like something out of a dream to Natalia. She wished she could see him sooner, but both her work and school precluded it. Not only did she have an intense modeling shoot in Harlem, but she had her demanding portfolio class to prepare for over the next three days too.

As her favorite part of *Messiah*—the choir singing Isaiah 9:6—started to play on the stereo, Natalia reached over for her remote control and turned it up. She could never hear those beautiful, prophetic words the prophet Isaiah penned several hundred years before Christ's birth without chills running up and down her spine.

" 'For unto us a child is born, unto us a son is given,' " she sang along with the choir and wished her voice could do it justice.

" 'And his name shall be called Wonderful, Counsellor, The mighty God, The everlasting Father, The Prince of Peace!' "

Natalia stopped singing as the words moved over and around her, and the Spirit within seemed to guide her in how to help Noel start his study of Jesus' names.

Isaiah 9:6. Handel's wonderful oratorio *Messiah*.

Scrambling to her feet, she ran over and picked up the newspaper. She flipped to the entertainment section. She was certain she'd seen it listed there. A special performance with opera stars was to be given one night soon at Carnegie Hall. But it was sold-out. That didn't deter Natalia. Picking up her phone, she dialed her agent's number. If anybody had spare tickets, it would be David. She glanced at her watch. It was late, but then he hardly ever slept.

When his cheery voice answered, she knew she was correct in calling him, even at such a late hour. "David, it's Natalia. I need a favor. . . ."

After talking with him for scarcely thirty seconds, she hung up the phone, then picked up a pillow and hugged it to her chest. It was done. As she'd expected, David had tickets, which he'd happily offered to her. He usually bought extra tickets for special events for his clients. Also, as she had expected, they were the best seats in the house.

Natalia knew now how she could help Noel in his search. She would let the wonder of the Christmas season and the wondrous truths heralded so perfectly in Handel's monumental work speak to Noel's heart. With God's Holy Spirit going about His holy business and the music filling Noel's being, it had to be a combination that would work.

It just had to!

❧

Three days later, while the earth still slept in 4:00 A.M. slumber, and Natalia did too, the phone by her bed rang out shrilly.

Reaching over to her table, she fumbled around for the noisy contraption. "Happy birthday, sleepyhead!" Noel's voice sounded as cheery as a robin singing in the spring.

"Noel! Happy birthday to you too!" she croaked and, pushing her hair away from her eyes, tried to focus on the numbers displayed on her clock. When she saw what time it was, she gasped. "Noel!"

"I know—I know. I said I'd come and get you at six. But something has changed."

Alarm filled her. "You won't be able to make it?" She had been looking forward to this morning with the same anticipation she normally reserved for Christmas and Easter.

"Not at all—just the opposite. We need to leave earlier than planned if we're going to get the full benefit of the wonderful gift to us today, the anniversary of the day of our births."

She shook her head, trying to wake up. "What are you talking about?"

"Put your feet on the floor, walk over to your window, and look out."

Carrying the phone with her, she did as he instructed. She pulled back the curtains and was instantly wide-awake because of what she saw. "Noel!"

" 'The moon on the breast of the new-fallen snow gave a luster of midday to objects below. . . ,' " he quoted. She recognized part of the poem *The Night Before Christmas*.

"Oh, Noel," she whispered into the phone. Her eyes took

in the beauty of the park covered in a glistening blanket of the purest white. "The first snow of the season. . ."

"And in time for our birthdays."

"Thank You, God." She whispered her thanks to the One she credited with this minor miracle.

"It is rather amazing, isn't it? Especially after our conversation the other night at the restaurant." But before she could reply he quickly said, "Tell me how it looks from your window."

She didn't hesitate. "Like a pristine world that's at once familiar and yet so utterly unfamiliar. I can see the tops of the buildings across the park, but they look as if they are floating above the trees, not connected to the ground at all." She squinted. "Almost as if they aren't really there." She gazed at the trees directly across from her window and placed her fingertips against the windowpane, not minding that it was freezing. "And the branches that seemed so bare yesterday are now covered by garments made to fit each of them perfectly. Like haute couture."

Her voice lowered to a whisper. "And it's so quiet, Noel. Even the light from the park lamps glowing among the branches seems to be hushed." She gave a little laugh. "As if light can be described as hushed. But it is." She paused. "There is no noise, Noel. No noise from the city at all. Everything is hushed with a serenity, a beauty, a solitude that is at once so humbling I feel as if I'm in the most beautiful cathedral in the world, and it makes me want to fall to my knees and pray. And yet"—she took a deep breath—"it is so thrilling too that I want to shout for joy. Oh, Noel! I've never seen the city look so perfect!"

"Few have, Natalia," he responded softly, and she could

hear the smile in his voice. "Can you and Prince be ready in twenty minutes, birthday girl?"

She glanced down at Prince. He lifted his head from his mat and cocked it to the side in question. "Prince already has his coat on. We'll be ready and waiting for you, birthday boy!"

seven

Exactly twenty minutes later, looking every inch the abominable snowman, Noel stood at the entrance to her building. He was covered from the top of his head to the toes of his boots in snow.

Natalia giggled at the sight of him.

When Roswell, the doorman, allowed him inside, an icy blast of air shot into the relative warmth of the hall. Without pausing, Noel reached out for her, picked her up, and twirled her around. She couldn't keep from squealing in delight.

"Happy birthday, birthday girl!" he said.

"Happy birthday, Noel," she returned softly in his ear. The smell of the snow on his shoulders was clean and fresh and cold.

She could have stayed in his arms forever, but Prince wasn't so certain about the situation. Noel as a "snowman" was not a familiar sight to him. When a soft growl emanated from the four-footed friend, Noel stopped twirling her and put her down.

"It's okay, Prince," she assured the dog. "He's a *friend*." He listened to her words, and she knew he understood the term "friend" from the way his head tilted to the side; but still it was obvious from his stance that he wasn't convinced. Only when Noel removed his glove and held out his hand so Prince could identify his scent did he relax. His tail started brushing back and forth in happiness over seeing Noel again too.

Natalia praised him. "Good boy, Prince. Good boy."

"That beast takes his job seriously," Roswell said from behind them.

"That he does," Natalia agreed, then turned to Noel to introduce the two men. "Noel, I'd like for you to meet the best doorman in New York City as well as a dear friend." Then to Roswell she said, "Noel is not only a very special person in my life—one you may let in whenever he comes calling—but it is his birthday today as well as my own."

"Oh!" the older man exclaimed. "That it is. The first day of Advent." He looked at Noel. "And it's your birthday too?"

"For the last twenty-eight years," Noel replied.

"Isn't that fine? You share the same day. Very special. And Advent too." He pointed to the snow that was swirling around the streetlights like a dancing troupe of white moths. "And you have the first snow of the season as a gift sent straight from God. A happy birthday to you both!"

"Thank you, Roswell." Then pointing to the key the older man held with uncertainty within his large hand, Natalia said, "You'd better do as I say and go up to my apartment and rest. Your wife doesn't need a sick husband for Christmas this year too."

Before Noel arrived, Natalia learned that Roswell had been unable to return home the previous night because of the snow, but his replacement had made it in. So she offered him the use of her apartment while she was gone. She could tell that reminding him of his illness the previous Christmas was all the encouragement the older man, who should have retired years ago, needed. He loved his wife dearly and never wanted to cause her distress.

"You are so right. Mary deserves me well this year," he said. "Thank you. I will take you up on your offer, Miss

Natalia. But if I fall asleep, you must promise to wake me the minute you step through the door."

"I promise," she replied. She knew the older man had a code of ethics that would be disturbed at the thought of her being in the apartment while he slept. She understood it perfectly; it was how men in Kastro, her *baba* included, would feel.

"Now at least I know why it had to snow so hard last night," the older man continued as if a mystery had been solved. "The good Lord has blessed this, the anniversary of your birthdays. You two young people are about to enjoy New York as few do. My Mary and I once went to the park early in the morning on the first snowfall of the season. But that was when we were as young and strong as you," he said. A special gleam came into his eyes as he recalled that time. Then he continued. "Central Park will be more marvelous right now than you have ever seen it before." With a flourish, he opened the door so the three of them could go on their way. "Have a wonderful time! And a very, very happy birthday to both of you!"

Roswell's words about the park being "marvelous" were correct, Natalia thought. It was that and so much more.

They shuffled through half a foot of the fluffy crystals that had settled on the avenue's sidewalk and stuck out their tongues like children to catch the new flakes as they fell from the sky. Soon they walked through one of the park's many gates and found themselves in a winter wonderland of delight that took their breath away on puffs of joy.

Were they in the park she knew so well? Natalia wondered. They walked with hushed steps across terrain she at once recognized yet didn't. It was as if Someone were sprinkling a deep layer of powdered sugar over the park, reminding her of the Greek Christmas cookies *Kourabiedes*.

She'd gone out at the first snowfall in Kastro many times and trekked up to the castle with her father, Martha, and older brothers several mornings to watch the sun rise over the white world of rural wonder.

But this was different.

This was New York City.

They were standing in the middle of one of the biggest cities in the world, and yet it was as if no one else existed.

Noel, Prince, and she were alone in a landscape as unfamiliar with its white pearly covering as it was familiar in its layout. She looked around as if she'd never seen these surroundings before. *Perhaps I haven't*, she thought. *Not in this light.* The character of the land had been transformed, made more perfect somehow—cleaner, smoother, crisper. She could hardly believe she had been living above these same trees for six winters but had never seen them looking quite like this before.

"Oh, Noel," she whispered and watched her words float to him on a wisp of icy breath. "Have you ever seen anything more excellent?" she asked as her boots crunched through the snow. It felt like a crime to mar the smooth path with her footsteps, as if she were trampling on something holy.

They were standing so close they were almost touching. "It's as if the snow has created the perfect landscape," he said, pointing out different things to her. "Look at the branches of the trees, the earth, the little creek with its stones that look like powder puffs with the snow piled upon them." He swept his arm up to the tall, ghostlike buildings that rose above this "rural" scene. "Even those structures look as if they're an illusion and not places where thousands of people are sleeping." He paused. Natalia took her gaze off Central Park in the predawn, snow-painted day and turned to him. "But most of all," he said, glancing at her curiously, "it's as if the great Artist Himself has reached down from heaven and with a palette of pure white re-created the world exactly as He might wish it to be. Pure, without anything to mar it, nothing to blemish it."

Searching his eyes, she saw sincerity in their depth as well as a clear vibrancy that she thought must come to a person when he recognized Truth. She was almost certain God's creation was speaking to Noel's soul.

She spoke softly. " 'For since the creation of the world God's invisible qualities—his eternal power and divine nature—have been clearly seen, being understood from what has been made, so that men are without excuse.' "

"That's in the Bible?" Noel asked. She heard awe in his voice.

Slowly, reverently, she nodded. "The New Testament. The Book of Romans."

He took a deep breath, one that made his chest expand, before turning back to the vista of trees and fields and hills that stretched out before them like a silk painting. "Something about this moment, Natalia," he whispered, "makes me feel as if that and everything you said at the restaurant about Jesus being God couldn't be anything but real." He sighed. "It's as if all this were created for our eyes alone." He shrugged his shoulders. "But I know it wasn't. It's for any of the millions of people in this great city who make the choice to get up early and come out and see it. Come out and see how God, during the restful night, has painted this special spot of His earth."

He turned to her again, and his gaze searched her own, as if he were trying to pull knowledge, her knowledge, from her. Like at the restaurant, it was something she wished to give freely.

"Isn't that like what you said the other night about human beings' choice? This"—he waved his hand out but didn't remove his eyes from hers—"is here for all the people in this city. Not just us. It's perfect right now, the best I've ever seen it; and yet I've never bothered, never made the choice, to get up early enough to come and experience it."

"It's exactly like that, Noel." She paused and smiled. "Except God doesn't require us to lose sleep when we make the decision to believe Him."

"Natalia," he breathed out her name. Wrapping his gloved hand gently around the back of her head, he slowly, respectfully, leaned down and brushed his lips against hers.

She closed her eyes.

She didn't think anything she'd ever felt, not even the warmth of the Grecian sun upon her skin in the summertime, was better than that of Noel's lips on hers. It was right and good and brilliant in the way she had always thought the kiss from her "Prince Charming" should be. And she knew she would never want to join her lips with another man's again.

Seemingly of its own volition, her mouth moved against his, and the motion deepened into a dance like a ballet of warmth and love.

"Natalia," Noel whispered against her lips, "I love you. With all my heart I do."

"And I love you," she heard herself respond and knew, even as the declaration sent her pulse spinning, that it was true. She couldn't have kept the truth of it from him any more than she could have kept the snow from swirling like a perfect dream around their heads.

They stood with their foreheads and noses resting together, making a silhouette of a heart with their profiles—that complete heart that could only be made by a couple in love. It was a romantic picture often represented on greeting cards with a sunset behind the couple. Natalia liked the fact that they had a sunrise.

After a moment Noel took a half step back and smiled, that all-encompassing smile of a man content with his world. She knew her smile had to match his. Her pulse was beating so fast she was certain he could see it move in her temple. She was just beginning to wonder where they would go from here in their relationship when he suddenly grabbed hold of her hand and started running.

"Come on!"

"Where are we going?" she squealed out as their boots crunched over snow.

"Somewhere special," he said and laughed. "You'll see!"

Prince pranced all around them, first kicking up the snow, then plowing through it like a burrowing animal building a tunnel. Letting go of one another's hands, they reached down, scooped it up, and tossed it at one another as they frolicked down the cozy, lamplit path. But when they reached a certain point and were ready to drop from their merry-making, they sat for a moment. They were panting as hard as Prince.

When Noel removed his scarf from around his neck, she looked at him in question. "Are you hot?" Playing had warmed her but not enough to be without her scarf. Central Park this morning was as freezing as it was beautiful.

"I want you to see the place I'm taking you from a certain vantage point. And I don't want you to look at it until then. So I want to tie this around your eyes and guide you there."

She looked out over the park. Except for the tall buildings surrounding it in the distance, it looked like a wilderness. But she trusted Noel. This would make it more of an adventure and more fun. "Okay," she agreed and, turning slightly, let him fix it. "Umm, the scarf is warm from your neck." It felt good. Her skin was tingling from the cold bite of morning air. "But I want to hold Prince close to me. Prince!" she called to the dog, who immediately stopped his snowplowing and came to her side. She attached his lead and wrapped her arm around him. "What a good boy you are," she cooed into his ear.

"And me?" she heard Noel ask from behind her as he secured the knot that held the scarf. "Am I a good boy?"

She reached out her arms and brought his face close to hers. "No. You aren't a good boy. You're a good man."

"Hmm." She could hear the pleasure in his voice and was sure his head had tilted to the side, as Prince's often did. "I like that. Come on." He reached for her right hand. "Let me show you the most perfect spot in all of Central Park."

They walked quietly down the path.

Seeing the white world was one thing, but feeling it and hearing it now that her eyes were blindfolded was another thing altogether. The snow crunched beneath their feet while her nose lifted and sniffed. She loved the way snow smelled. It was a clean, fresh scent, the same whether it fell in the wilds of Kastro or in the middle of this city of concrete and steel. But never had it smelled or felt better than it did now. She had never walked through the snow with the man she loved. She hugged Noel's arm closer to her.

He chuckled, and she knew he was looking at her when he asked, "Are you scared?"

"No, I just like the excuse to hold you close."

He paused. And she knew a moment before it happened that his lips were going to touch hers. She sensed them coming close. "I like it too." His voice was deep and husky. "But you don't ever need an excuse. That, dear Natalia, is something you are welcome to do for no reason at all."

Natalia placed her head on his shoulder. She hadn't known that to be so close to a man would feel so good. She was aware of the muscles beneath his coat as he moved, the way his breathing sounded, the soft scent of his aftershave, and even his height as he crunched along beside her. It made her feel warm and toasty and feminine.

"We're here," Noel said after a few minutes and situated her in a certain direction. "Stay like that," he said as he undid the scarf. "And keep your eyes closed until I tell you to open them."

"You're certainly full of orders," she teased.

"Not usually." She could hear the smile in his voice. "There—got it." As the scarf fell away, a sharp, sudden chill stung her skin, but she hardly noticed it as she concentrated on Noel and his surprise. "Not yet, not yet," he spoke slowly. She felt as if he were a cameraman telling her to hold a pose until the lighting was perfect.

"Now!"

She blinked her eyes.

"Oh!" She couldn't help the gasp that came from her at the vista before her. The little Gothic castle, Belvedere, which sat on a rocky outcropping to the west had always been one of her favorite places to visit—probably because of the castle in Kastro. But she had never seen it looking like this.

To the east and behind them, the dawning sun had found an opening in the clouds. It highlighted the castle with golden light even as snow still swirled around it like laughter falling from the sky. Natalia half expected to see a rainbow appear at any moment.

And one did!

Shafts of sunlight lit up the blanket of snow in the glen before the castle, and the snow sparkled like that of a rainbow in the sky.

"Oh, Noel," she breathed out. "It's enchanting."

"Perfect for our fairy-tale romance?" he asked.

Turning from the castle to him and with her heart thudding heavily in her chest, she wrapped her arms around his neck. "Absolutely perfect."

He reached out and tucked a strand of her hair that had come loose from her hat back under the fabric. "Happy birthday, Natalia."

"Happy birthday, Noel," she whispered back.

"It's been perfect."

"And it's not even six o'clock in the morning yet!"

He nodded toward a man walking from the opposite direction. "I'm glad we came out so early and got to see the castle like this. Now that the sun is coming up, the park will soon be filled with joggers, dog walkers, and even cross-country skiers out to practice their technique." Noel squinted toward the man who was cutting a wide arc so as not to disturb the pristine snowscape. "But I think that man is here to try to capture this moment forever for a book or a calendar."

Natalia looked at the man. The camera equipment he had strung across his shoulders told its own tale. "He might capture the scene," she agreed. "But one can only experience the moment, the enchantment, by coming here into God's world and feeling it. It is so special, so ethereal, so—"

"A part of God?"

That was exactly what it was. "Do you feel it, Noel?" she

whispered. "Do you feel God speaking to your soul through this encounter with His creation?"

"I do, Natalia. It's something I feel here." He tapped his chest. "I know God exists. I just don't know Him as I'm realizing I should." He sighed. "I wanted to tell you today that I started my study of Jesus' names. But I didn't know where to begin, even though I've found my Bible and have it on my bedside table now."

"I thought that might happen," she said softly.

"You did?" His chin lifted a fraction of an inch in reaction to the news. "How?"

How can I explain it to him? she wondered. *"The way it actually is,"* a voice replied within her. So she did. "It's just something God put into my heart."

"Really?"

She nodded. "I think you'll soon see how He does that."

"Do you think so? I want that. I want what you have and my parents have. . ."

"That want is God knocking on the door of your heart, Noel. ' "Here I am!" ' Jesus says in His revelation to John. ' "I stand at the door and knock. If anyone hears my voice and opens the door, I will come in and eat with him, and he with me." ' " She gazed out over the beautiful park. "It's the way you hear His 'voice' here today."

"That's beautiful," Noel murmured. "I'm beginning to see the Bible is a very poetic book. Every line seems to contain music."

Her heart beat faster. "Do you like music, Noel?"

"Love it. Especially classical composers."

"Yippee!" she exclaimed and laughed.

Noel looked at her as if she had gone mad, but she couldn't help it. She was so happy. Reaching into her pocket, she pulled out an envelope she had decorated with a length of candy-cane-colored yarn and gave it to him.

"Here," she said. "This is my birthday present to both of us."

"To *both* of us?" he countered, with an amused lift of his dark brow.

"They go together like the celebration of our birthdays does."

As the world slowly started filling with people—the joggers, dog walkers, and cross-country skiers Noel had anticipated—he removed the yarn from the envelope and pulled out two tickets. He turned them over, read them, then looked back at her. "Natalia. . .Handel's *Messiah*. . .I don't know what to say." So he didn't say anything else with words; rather, his face bent toward hers and touched his lips lightly to hers. She wrapped her arms around his neck and rested her head against his shoulder.

"I think you just 'said' everything perfectly, Noel," Natalia whispered.

eight

With the first sounds of the orchestra, Noel knew he was in for an experience he'd never had before.

Normally he was a visual person. But this performance of Handel's *Messiah* was already making him use his sense of hearing unlike any time before. And that sense seemed to demand that another one was to be employed, different from the five physical senses he was so accustomed to relying upon.

As the notes filled the air around them, Noel glanced over at Natalia.

Her eyes were closed. Her lips were moving as if in prayer.

It was something Noel almost felt like doing.

When the tenor sang the first word, "Comfort," Noel smiled to himself. What a poignant way to start a work titled *Messiah*. Nearly everyone needed comfort in some form or another.

Noel sat back in his seat. But as the music combined with the wonderful words, he found himself leaning forward. The Word of God, which he hadn't known how to start reading a few nights earlier, was proclaimed so beautifully by some of the world's most highly trained voices. What struck Noel too was that they sung only the words written in the Bible.

Nothing else.

And those words did things to Noel.

They stirred him in a way he had never been moved before.

When the choir sang, " 'And the glory of the LORD shall be revealed,' " it made Noel want to stand up and sing with them. A thrill went through him. It was as if a chorus of angels were on stage glorifying the Lord.

He didn't understand what they meant by "all flesh shall see together." But he wanted to find out.

The bass singer came in with the words, " 'He will shake the heavens and the earth,' " like thunder giving an exclamation to what had been sung. " 'The LORD, whom ye seek, shall suddenly come to his temple' " was like a wake-up call to Noel. Something like tears formed at the back of Noel's eyes when the bass singer asked, " 'But who may abide the day of his coming? and who shall stand when he appeareth?' " Noel wondered if he would be able to. He suspected that, as he was now, he would neither abide nor stand when the "He" they referred to, Jesus the Christ, the Messiah, should appear.

" 'He is like a refiner's fire' " sounded ominous to Noel.

" 'But who may abide the day of his coming?' " the singer repeated the question, and Noel, like a child, wanted to shout out that he would. He would stand! But to do so he thought he had to learn how first, like a child learning to stand on his feet for the first time.

The choir came in singing so sweet and calming, like a rest after the bass's ominous question. But what was this angelic-type choir saying? Noel leaned forward to catch the words. " 'He shall purify.' "

Whom shall he purify?

" 'The sons of Levi,' " the choir seemed to answer him, "offer unto the LORD an offering in righteousness." Noel wondered who the sons of Levi were and what they had to do with him. It sounded like a glorious hope to him, though.

But wait! What was the alto proclaiming now?

" 'Shall call his name' "—His *name*—" 'Emmanuel: God with us.' "

Emmanuel. God with us! She sang it only once, and for a moment Noel wondered if he had heard correctly.

He glanced over at Natalia. Her face was glowing with a light that had nothing to do with that found in the dimly lit auditorium. It was a light shining from her face.

" 'Behold your God!' " the alto sang. " 'The glory of the LORD is risen upon thee.' " And Noel knew that was exactly what was upon Natalia. The glory of the Lord had risen upon her face. Noel looked around him. On so many faces— Caucasian faces, African faces, Oriental faces, Indian faces. And yet they all looked the same, almost as if light was upon them, and it in turn was shining out from their souls!

The choir sang the same words, " 'The glory of the LORD is risen upon thee!' " It was joyously sung, and Noel's heart thumped to its glorious beat.

Then the bass sang again. A soulful sound of sadness. Noel listened to his words and realized he sounded so sad because the words he recited were sad. " 'For, behold, darkness shall cover the earth, and gross darkness the people.' "

'Gross darkness?' Was that how he was? Was he living in gross darkness by not getting to know God the way his parents knew Him? He glanced over at the woman he loved. The way Natalia knew Him? He looked at others seated around him. The way so many people in this auditorium apparently knew Him?

The music changed again, and Noel felt expectation in the melody, though still sad, that now diffused throughout the room. " 'The LORD shall arise upon thee. Upon thee, and his glory shall be seen upon thee! The people that walked in darkness have seen a great light! Have seen a great light!' "

Yes! Noel sang within himself.

Light!

That was it!

The people around me—Natalia, my parents—they have seen a great light, a light Noel was beginning to realize he wanted to see.

" 'And they that dwell in the land of the shadow of death"—Noel had heard his parents refer to that phrase often—"upon them hath the light shined.' "

With shock Noel realized the Light referred to must be Christ, the Messiah, the Son of God, the Light of the World! He knew that was one of Jesus' names. People didn't have to be an expert on the names of Jesus to know that one.

The choir lifted up their many voices in song again with a part of this work Noel had heard many times but had never listened to before. It permeated every corner of the hall.

" 'For unto us a child is born, unto us a son is given: and the government shall be upon his shoulder, and his name shall be called Wonderful! Counsellor! The mighty God! The everlasting Father! The Prince of Peace!' "

Noel felt goose bumps break out over him.

Names!

Christ's glorious names filled the hall.

Names of the Man—the God—Natalia and his parents wanted him to understand. Amazing names. Descriptive names. Significant names. Names for him to study and help him know the character of the Man, the God, who meant so much to so many people he loved.

He glanced over at Natalia.

She turned her gold-crowned head to him and reached for his hand. "His names," she mouthed. He knew then why she had bought these tickets for them.

Nodding, he smiled. And chills of wonder, of hope, flowed through him because he knew the only barrier between this woman and him having the life together they both so desired was his faith. He was beginning to think that along with his lack of faith—though he had always believed in God—was a lack of knowledge about the nature of God, about who God is. He could read and study, and he had ignored probably the most important book ever given to the world. The Bible. The Word of God. The Word these beautiful voices were proclaiming a small portion of so magnificently and mightily.

The choir sang in allegro. As before, Noel wished he could sing with them. His soul yearned to sing the declaration, the praise, the acknowledgment.

" 'Wonderful!' "

" 'Counsellor!' "

" 'The mighty God!' "

" 'The everlasting Father!' "

" 'The Prince of Peace!' "

Something inside him jumped to the fullness of the resounding sound. He wanted to hear it over and over again.

And yet, even when it ended, which seemed too soon, he found he couldn't be sad. For the pastoral symphony that followed the chorus was like a gentle caress on the excitement of his soul. One that gave him the chance to rest and listen to the remainder of the story.

Noel now had several names to study: Emmanuel, Light, Wonderful, Counsellor, the Mighty God, the Everlasting Father, and the Prince of Peace.

All names that described the Person of Christ.

He glanced over at Natalia, who was dressed in a sequined gown of soft, royal blue that winked and blinked with her movement. She turned and looked at him. He knew he didn't have to tell her how he felt. She could see it.

And he was certain it pleased her.

When the soprano started singing again, they turned their gazes toward the front, but their hands remained intertwined as the words flowed around them and through them.

" 'There were shepherds abiding in the field, keeping watch over their flock by night.' " Noel knew this. It was the Christmas story. " 'And the angel said unto them: Fear not: for, behold, I bring you good tidings of great joy, which shall be to all people. For unto you is born this day in the city of David a Saviour, which is Christ the Lord.' "

Savior! Christ the Lord! More names! Noel's mind reverberated with the belief that was supplanting the disbelief within him.

" 'Glory to God in the highest!' " the female members of the choir sang. " 'And peace on earth!' " the men returned. When they started singing in a round, exhilaration filled Noel. " 'Good will to men!' " The many voices, both male and female in turn, overflowed into the room, with a joyful noise that seemed to seep into every pore of Noel's body. He felt himself break out into a light sweat, an amazing thing considering the snow that covered the ground outside.

" 'Rejoice greatly,' " the soprano sang, sounding like bells chiming, like Natalia's laughter. " 'Behold, thy King cometh unto thee. . .speak peace unto the heathen.' "

Heathen. The word stuck in Noel's brain. For the first time he realized belief in God was not enough. Belief in a

Supreme Being made him little more than a heathen. There was much, much more to belief than believing in God.

The words *"Yes, belief in God's redemptive work through His Son"* marched through his brain. He wasn't sure when he had heard them, but he thought they were probably some of the many bits of knowledge he'd picked up from his parents through the years. Before this evening they were just words; now they were so much more. Now they were truth. A truth Noel was coming to accept.

" 'Then shall the eyes of the blind be opened, and the ears of the deaf unstopped; then shall the lame man leap as an hart, and the tongue of the dumb sing.' " That was what Noel was feeling at this moment, as if he were seeing and hearing and his heart was jumping in knowledge of God's greatness for the first time. And like a man who had never had the use of his tongue, he wanted to speak it out and sing it out too! The thought went through his mind that he had been dumb for years because he hadn't bothered to proclaim truth, the truth of God.

But what was the alto saying now? What truth was coming forth from the notes of her mouth? " 'He shall feed his flock like a shepherd: he shall gather the lambs with his arm.' " The imagery was beautiful.

And now the soprano sang, " 'He will give you rest!' " Noel wanted that. The choir was singing the best sermon he'd ever heard. The music was moving his heart in a direction he'd long yearned to travel but, at the same time, had long fought to go.

" 'And ye shall find rest unto your souls.' " Noel recognized that rest for his soul was something he'd never had. Oh, he didn't have any major problems—he wasn't an unhappy person at all—but there had always been an unease, as if he were missing out on something in his life, something great.

The choir came in now, singing words that sounded like a springtime dance of delight, reminding Noel of butterflies flittering around daisies. " 'His yoke is easy; his burden is light!' " And he smiled. Almost laughed.

" 'Behold the Lamb of God,' " the choir now sang in largo. Noel knew he was hearing another name of Christ's, one he'd heard as a child in Sunday school. *Jesus, the Lamb of God.* He recalled the lambs in his Sunday school coloring books, lambs with Jesus in the picture.

The next words filled Noel with sadness. "He is despised and rejected of men: a man of sorrows, and acquainted with grief." But when Noel realized he was one of those men who had rejected Him by simply ignoring Him, by not believing all His words, only a select few, the grief and sorrow and conviction that filled him were nearly overwhelming. The section was so long and slow he thought Handel had probably written it like that for a reason: to give each man and woman time to let the full import of the words sink into their souls.

They sunk deeply into Noel's. Very deeply.

Sadness filled him as he realized by his lack of interest in God's Son he had, in fact, rejected Him. He hadn't taken the time to get acquainted with Him or, as Natalia had pointed out that night at the restaurant, to learn all about what Jesus said while He was on earth as a Man.

Here he was, a counselor, always advising parents and children to get to know one another. God had given everything for people to do that, but Noel had spent the first twenty-eight years of his life practically ignoring Him.

As the sad, convicting words filled the glamorous hall, Noel remembered his father telling him once, "God has given us everything we need to know Him. He has given His

Son, His Holy Spirit, His Word to hold in our hands and read, the testimony of men and women from the earliest days of Christianity to the present as witnesses and examples of true belief. All that plus the gift of volition. God, the Builder and Designer of the infinite universe and the smallest leaf on a tree, has left it up to us whether we puny, sinful humans want to know Him or not."

Noel felt a keen sense of conviction upon remembering his father's words and hearing the current ones sung in the auditorium.

He suspected that George Frideric Handel must have loved God very much to write such inspirational combinations of sounds to go to the arrangement of biblical words.

That was Noel's thought when the music stopped and the lights in the auditorium flicked on for intermission.

As people all around them arose from their seats, Noel and Natalia continued to sit in silence.

Finally, when he could speak, he admitted to her, "I am speechless." He squeezed her hand gently and whispered, "It is so wonderful, so convicting." He touched his free hand to his heart. "I have so much learning to do, so many decisions to make."

"Only one decision, dear Noel," she corrected him quietly.

He nodded slowly. "Yes," he agreed. "Only one."

After the intermission the music continued to wash over Noel. When the choir in magnificent allegro broke into singing, " 'Hallelujah, for the Lord God omnipotent reigneth,' " Noel felt something sacred was happening.

He thought he'd been moved earlier when the choir had sung, "For unto us a son is given." But it was nothing compared to the emotions that filled him on hearing the voices of the men and women when they praised God in this refrain. He was not even surprised when everyone—like a giant wave—stood up for the words filling the airwaves of the room. The question would have been, how could anyone not stand in the face of such a magnificent sound of praise? It was the most heavenly sound Noel had ever heard, and he imagined angels taking part in the singing. It was too beautiful to belong only in the human realm.

As the glorious combination of words and music rose higher and higher, a majestic crescendo proclaiming glory to the one and only God of heaven and earth and to the Messiah, the Christ, who is One and the same God, Noel's unlearned heart cried out to believe in Jesus as God's one and only Son.

To the " 'King of Kings, and Lord of Lords!' "

For these were not words composed by men but glorious truths God had given men of things to come. At that moment as the choir sang, " 'The kingdoms of this world are become the kingdoms of our Lord, and of his Christ,' " Noel knew it was the truth. " 'He shall reign for ever and ever! He shall reign for ever and ever! King of Kings, and Lord of Lords!' " Noel knew this to be true too, and he wanted to live under that rule. He didn't want to be left behind or not allowed to be present when the King of the universe reigned, simply because he hadn't taken the time to know God's Son now— while he had the chance.

The choir ended, again too soon for Noel, and the people sat down to experience the rest of the prophetic and inspired words Handel had set to music. Noel resolved not to tell Natalia about his decision yet. It was something personal between him and God and too new for him to share even with the woman he loved. He still wanted to learn about the names of Christ. Then he'd tell her he finally under-stood that, to be one of God's children, a person must believe in God as well as acknowledge that Jesus is the Christ, the Messiah.

He looked over at her as the chorus of amens was sung and smiled.

It was enough to know that because of his decision, his new and as yet unrevealed one, he and this most wonderful of women now had the prospect of a future together. Because second only to his new relationship with the Lord Jesus Christ—which he somehow knew must always hold first place in his heart, in the hearts of all humans—was his rela-tionship with this woman. Next to God and his parents, she was becoming the most important person in his life.

And he prayed, yes, prayed, as she turned her sparkling blue eyes upon him, that they would be granted a long and lovely life together.

nine

It was snowing again—bright, fanciful flakes that flittered and danced around their heads—when they walked out the doors of the concert hall.

"It's wonderful!" Natalia laughed and held out her ungloved hand to the crystals. Surprisingly, for something so cold, they only seemed to add warmth to the ambience of the night. She felt Noel's arm go around her shoulder, and she gladly snuggled against his side.

"This has been one of the most wonderful nights of my life, if not the very best," he said. She didn't think she'd ever been happier.

"Me too, Noel. I'm so glad you enjoyed the oratorio."

" 'Enjoyed' is not the word to describe what I was feeling in there," he admitted, and she said a silent prayer of thanks for his declaration. She thought it had moved him. She only wondered to what extent.

He guided her over to the line of people waiting for a taxi. He paused and looked up at the swirling snow falling from the nighttime sky. She waited without comment, allowing him the time to speak his thoughts, as he had so often allowed her. "It was almost as if. . .the door to my heart were somehow opened, as if those wonderful words somehow drew me near to God. I don't know. Here's yet another metaphor for you." He looked at her. "I felt almost as if God were embracing my soul as my father used to hug me when I was a little boy. Does that make any sense to you?"

"Perfect sense," she replied, watching their frosted breaths mingle together and wrap around their heads like a happy cloud. "Jesus said, ' "But I, when I am lifted up from the earth, will draw all men to myself." ' "

"That's it!" Noel exclaimed softly. "I feel as if I want to learn all about Him and that I can believe everything Jesus told us when He was here on earth, even that He is God."

She didn't say a word but wrapped her arms around him and squeezed the man she loved close to her. Their heavy wool coats were between them, but it didn't matter.

Wool was just material.

What had been between them before—Noel's lack of belief in Jesus as God's Son and as God—was something she could not have taken away herself. Only the anointing and urging of the Holy Spirit could do that. And faith.

The change she sensed in Noel was as pure and wonderful and refreshing as the snow that danced around them and settled upon their heads, their shoulders, the ground upon which they stood, as well as the lighted building tops that soared into the sky above the city of New York.

To say it was a magical moment would be to take something away from God.

There was no magic involved.

This was a God-sent moment, one of those special instances where eternity and time seem to make everything still and sweet and as similar to heaven as people on earth can come to it. It was a passionate moment but one that had nothing to do with the passions of the body, rather, everything to do with the passions of the spirits, the souls, of two of God's children. For although Noel didn't say it, Natalia was almost certain he had made the most important decision a person could ever make, the one about Jesus, during the soaring sounds proclaiming His prophecies, life, work, death, resurrection, and future reign. Natalia was certain Noel was God's child by conscious choice now.

The verse "No one who denies the Son has the Father; whoever acknowledges the Son has the Father also" went through Natalia's head. Somehow she could sense the change in Noel; his spirit was no longer denying the Son His glorious place in the Godhead.

As much as she might want to, Natalia wouldn't press him for any more information right now. Neither God, her heavenly Father, nor her earthly father, her *baba*—the wisest person she knew in the ways of God—ever pressed a person; rather, they both waited until the person was ready on his or her own to speak.

Natalia would wait.

It was enough to feel this change, this heaven-sent change in the man she loved.

He turned and, with his nose almost touching her nose, said, "This feeling of belonging, of being drawn to something so right and good as what those words in there"—he pointed to the concert hall—"proclaimed, is like coming home after a very long absence. Almost as if I'd been lost but now am found."

"Dear Noel," she said, reaching up and touching the snowflakes that made his dark hair shine as if with stardust, "do you know you repeated some famous words in the Bible almost verbatim?"

He tilted his head to the side, and she knew he was waiting for her to continue.

"In the story about the prodigal son—"

"Wait," he interrupted her. "I know this story. From Sunday school when I was a little guy. It's about a man who takes his half of his father's inheritance and squanders it on immoral living. When he runs out and sees the pigs where he's working are eating better than he is, he realizes he must go home and apologize to his father."

She nodded. "And when he returned his father said, ' "Let's have a feast and celebrate. For this son of mine was dead and is alive again; he was lost and is found." ' "

Noel clicked his cheek thoughtfully. "That's another good metaphor to describe how I felt while listening to that music—how I still feel. I feel as though I was dead before, as if the life I led before this evening was almost totally different from the one I want to lead now."

If their turn for a taxi hadn't arrived then, Natalia wasn't so sure she could have kept from asking Noel what had happened to him during the concert, about the decision he'd made. But as she bent down and scooted into the warm cab, taking care not to muss her gown, she knew it had to be God's timing. Noel would tell her everything at the right moment.

But for now he had told her enough.

The man she loved was coming to know God. That's all she needed to see.

Noel instructed the driver to take them to the General Electric Building where he'd made reservations for them at the Rainbow Room. Reaching into his breast pocket he asked, "Do you mind if I turn on my phone? I'm concerned about Rachel, that student I told you about."

"Of course. Turn it on."

"I think she's at an intersection in her life now. She can either go the right way or— " He let out a deep sigh and smiled. "She should hear the *Messiah*."

"Do you know how many people's lives have been touched by it during the last two hundred and fifty years?" she asked.

Noel looked at her in surprise. "That long? I didn't realize Handel lived two hundred and fifty years ago."

Enjoying history as much as she did, Natalia studied things she particularly liked, so she knew a little about the composer. "Handel was born in Germany in the late 1600s and moved to England in the early 1700s. Ludwig van Beethoven said he was the greatest composer to have ever lived."

Noel's brows rose. "Beethoven said that?"

She nodded. "And most people considered Beethoven the greatest."

"I think if anybody should know, he would."

She smiled. "When Handel composed *Messiah* he was fifty-seven years old. But just before its success he was depressed, plagued by rheumatism that didn't allow him to sleep and afraid to answer his door for fear he'd be hauled off to debtors' prison."

He looked at her curiously. "Are you serious?"

"It's sad, but so many people who have given the world such mighty works or used their talents in one way or another have had very difficult lives. But I've always thought it might be something like the apostle Paul and his thorn. It made these very gifted people realize His 'grace *is* sufficient' for them, and it was the thorns that made people strive for new heights. Heights in writing, like people living under persecution, and in music like Handel's *Messiah*. God's grace was sufficient for them."

"I've never thought about it like that."

"I read that while composing *Messiah* Handel was said to have seen visions about the subjects he was writing, especially during the 'Hallelujah Chorus.'"

Noel whistled. "Now that's something I can believe."

"You can?"

"It was"—he held his hands out before him—"as if angels were singing."

She nodded thoughtfully. "The amazing thing, though, is that it portrays not angels, but humans who have come out of the Great Tribulation and are proclaiming the 'Lord God Almighty reigns' and He is the 'King of Kings and Lord of Lords.' It's a prophecy for us today, who wait for Christ's second coming, as much as what was written hundreds of years before the birth of Christ in Isaiah, 'For to us a child is born, to us a son is given,' was for those at the time of Christ's first coming."

He looked at her with the same admiration in his eyes she remembered seeing in her father's eyes for her mother. It made Natalia feel warm and cherished and adored. "You amaze me. How do you know all this?"

She shrugged. "My parents and family have tried to live by the Word of God—"

"I have had that too, though," he interrupted her. She knew it was true. His parents were believers.

"Yes, but I didn't fight what my parents taught me by their wise counsel as you have fought yours, Noel." When his gaze seemed to glaze over, she felt heat rise to her face as embarrassment flooded her. She took his hand in hers. "I'm so sorry, Noel. That sounded so pompous, so self-righteous. . . ."

"No." He reached up and touched her cheek. "It sounded only like honesty to me. I don't mind that."

"I don't want to hurt you."

"Don't you think I know that?"

"I just want you—"

"To 'get it'?" he asked.

"Do you?" she whispered. They were in a taxi zipping through midtown Manhattan, but the world seemed to stand still as she waited for his answer. "Has everything changed tonight?" she asked in spite of her best intentions not to press him. She was almost certain of it, though. Her spirit could sense it.

In less than a heartbeat he covered the few inches that separated them. And just before his lips touched hers he whispered, "My darling, I think you might count on it. . . ."

The kisses they had shared in Central Park had been special because they had been the first ones and given with a declaration of love. But this kiss was like a merging of souls going in the same direction. Natalia wished the moment to last forever.

But the trill of Noel's phone in his pocket would not allow it.

He pulled away and reached for the phone. "I sure hope that's a wrong number."

Glancing at the name on the screen, Noel frowned. "It's Rachel—that girl I told you about." He put the phone to his ear. "Rachel—" Natalia watched him raise his hand. "Wait a minute. Start from the beginning." It was clear the girl had a problem. More than the usual. Natalia leaned forward and sent up a prayer on the girl's behalf—and on Noel's that he would know what to do. "Yes, of course I can come." He gave Natalia a questioning look, as if to ask for permission.

"Of course," she whispered. Their plans to go to the Rainbow Room could wait for another night.

"Okay, where are you?" He glanced at his watch. "Sit tight. I'll be there in ten minutes." Ending the call, he turned to Natalia.

"I'm so sorry—"

Natalia stopped him. "Don't be. Is there anything I can do?"

A sheepish grin crossed his face. "I was counting on your asking. Would you mind coming with me? I make it a practice never to meet students away from the school alone. In this situation I would normally ask another counselor to accompany me, but I don't want to waste time. The girl sounded very frightened, and I'm afraid—"

"You don't need to explain," Natalia said, smiling. "I would be very happy to come with you."

"You're amazing, you know that?"

It thrilled her that he thought so. Reaching up, she placed her hand against his cheek. "Since you're the one who's going to the rescue of a disturbed teenager, I think *you're* the amazing one."

❧

Not ten minutes later they walked into the diner where Rachel sat slouched in the last booth in the corner. And Noel learned that Natalia was even more remarkable than he had thought.

Rachel looked up then and saw them approaching the table. The look of astonishment and pleasure that crossed her face on seeing Natalia was so out of character for the normally ill-tempered teenager that Noel thought she was a different girl. She seemed to change before him. She went from having eyes that resembled mud on a stormy day to ones that looked as bright as a travel brochure of Bali might.

"Oh! Oh! Oh!" The girl scrambled to her feet and stood before Natalia with barely constrained glee. "Mr. Sheffield, how did you know? How did you know?"

"Hello, Rachel," he heard Natalia say and was further surprised by the way she was unflustered by the girl's reaction to her, almost as if she were used to it.

"Audrey Shepherd!" the girl exclaimed. "You're my favorite! My absolutely favorite model! I want to be just like you. Oh, I know I don't look like you. I've got dark hair, and you're very blond. But, oh, I would love to be a model like you someday!"

"A model like you someday?" Noel heard the girl gush and knew she couldn't be referring to someone who modeled nurses' uniforms. That wasn't Rachel's style. The girl wore only the latest, most trendy, and expensive fashions on the market. For Rachel to react this way, Natalia had to do much more than "a bit of modeling." And much more than nurses' uniforms.

The way she carried herself, her expensive address, taking six years to complete the program at the university, her clothes. Yes, now that he thought about it, he should have known. There were other things too. The way people often looked at her, almost as if they knew her. It hadn't registered that they were looking at her that way because she was famous, rather than because of her lovely appearance.

But he couldn't be angry about her omission.

He understood it.

Hadn't he done the same thing by not telling her about his book that was now six weeks on the *New York Times* bestseller list?

Rachel stopped speaking and pressed her hand against her stomach. "I don't think that will ever happen now." She turned to Noel. "Mr. Sheffield, I think I might be pregnant."

Noel's eyes widened. He couldn't help it. He'd never had to deal with this area of counseling before. The female counselors at school took these cases. He'd known he might eventually confront it, but did it have to happen now, with Natalia present?

"Now calm down, Rachel," he said and motioned for the girl to be seated. "Are you sure you are? Have you seen a doctor?" He and Natalia sat down also. He was glad Natalia chose to sit next to the girl. In her gown of sequined jewels, which even the fluorescent lights in the diner caught flashing from between the folds of her cashmere coat, she might have looked out of place in the diner. But she didn't. She looked as wonderful as she had at the concert.

"No," Rachel mumbled, sounding like a six year old. He brought his attention back to the girl, rather than where he would prefer it to be, on Natalia.

"Then how can you be sure?" he heard himself ask.

"I'm not," she shot back sullenly. "But I'm late. And I'm never late." Her voice was hard, until she seemed to remember who was sitting next to her. She looked at Natalia and asked with a sugar-sweet voice, "What have you done when you've found yourself in this situation, Audrey?"

Audrey? Noel frowned then remembered. The girl had said Natalia's professional name. Audrey something—Audrey Shepherd. She must have chosen "Shepherd" for *German shepherd.*

He watched as Natalia took a breath. He wanted to hear the answer as much as the girl. Even though he knew Natalia, in light of her profession, he wondered how she *had* coped.

"Well, first of all, my real name is Natalia, and you may call me that," she said to the girl.

"Thanks." The girl looked down but not fast enough for Noel to miss seeing she was pleased by the honor.

"Second," Natalia continued, "I have *never* found myself in that situation, Rachel, because I have never been married."

"You've *never*—I mean—I didn't think models thought they had to be married before. . ."

Natalia smiled wryly. "Some, no, but as with all groups of people and professions, not all. Many are wise about their relationships. A few are not, and they are the ones by whom people judge all others."

"Wow! So you're—I mean—since you haven't been married before—that means you're a. . . ?" She let the last word trail off, but it was obvious what she was asking. Natalia smiled at the girl before she turned back to Noel.

"That's right," she responded. Noel was glad she answered him even if he hadn't asked—and would never have asked—such a thing.

He had known all along she was pure; he had sensed it the first time they spoke at the tree. But the way he felt upon hearing her words was as if she were handing him a gift.

"Wow!" Rachel repeated her earlier declaration. "That's amazing."

Natalia looked back at her. "Not really. What is, though, is that young men and women would do things that could forever alter their lives, either through illness or"—she paused and spoke more softly—"through bringing a child into the world."

Rachel moaned. "What am I going to do?"

"Have you talked to your parents about this?" Natalia asked.

"No way!" the girl exclaimed. "They'd tell me it was my fault, and they'd probably want me to get rid of it." Natalia cringed at her words. Noel could tell that Rachel saw her cringe too, because she was quick to assure Natalia. "But I couldn't. That's one thing I couldn't do. Even if being pregnant disfigured my body so I could never be a model, I would never do that."

"I'm glad." Natalia took the girl's hand in her own. "If you are pregnant, the Bible tells us God already knows your child and wouldn't want you to hurt him or her."

Rachel looked up at her with what Noel could only describe as awe. "Do you believe in God too?"

Natalia smiled and nodded her head. "Absolutely."

"If you believe in Him, He must be real. Would you teach me about Him? I think I need Him," the girl admitted.

Noel couldn't believe what he was hearing, but he knew it was true.

And he understood it.

It was simple really: Natalia's life was a witness to this young and impressionable girl.

He heard Natalia respond with an offer of friendship. "I would love to teach you about God." When a big smile spread across Rachel's face, Noel felt that, for the first time since meeting the troubled young student, she would be okay.

Where his counseling and talking had failed, Natalia and God would not. The witness of God in Natalia's life would turn the girl around.

Of that Noel was almost certain.

And it made him glad.

ten

Two evenings later Noel stood gazing into the miniature house—a perfect, doll-sized re-creation of the home in which he had been raised. Even the tree—the one that now graced Rockefeller Center—was included in the model. The Sheffield family would never forget it, especially Noel, because it had brought him and Natalia together.

All the miniature lights were lit in the dollhouse, giving it the warm, cozy feeling of Christmas. His mother had made tiny wreaths for every window as identical wreaths hung in the windows of the actual house.

Noel leaned down and peered into the replica of the comfortable den in which his parents and he now sat. A tree—similar to the one that stood in the corner beside the hearth—was there. Even dolls that represented his parents, him, and the two German shepherds that were lounging by the side of the fireplace were in their proper place. A miniature woman with soft platinum hair was sitting on her sofa. A man with wings of distinguished silver around his temples was ensconced on his recliner watching television. And a young man in slacks and a polo shirt stood looking at the replica of the dollhouse, which was even represented in the dollhouse itself.

Noel breathed out a sigh and turned to his mother. "I don't know how you did this. It's fantastic."

She laughed, a light tinkling sound that reminded him of Natalia. It wasn't identical, just flavored with the same pitch of happy humor. He suspected it probably had to do with his mother's and Natalia's faith. "To be truthful, I'm rather amazed I did it too."

"It was a labor of love," his father declared and gazed over at his wife. His face had that special look he reserved for the woman he loved.

His mother glanced around the room. "This home has given me much joy since the day I came to live here. I guess the model is a small way of returning some of the love I've felt within these walls since you two welcomed me and made me a part of it and a part of your lives." She placed the afghan she was crocheting to the side and reached out for the older Sheffield's hand, which was never too far away. "As your wife." She looked at Noel and sent him that wonderful look of a mother's love he had so craved when she and his father had first married and one he still treasured seeing. "And as your mother."

"It's Noel and I who have been blessed by your being here with us," the elder Sheffield was quick to respond, and Noel nodded. "I don't know what we men would have done without you, Jennifer. We would have rattled around this big, old house and driven one another nuts." His eyes twinkled in humor.

All three smiled.

They all knew they'd gotten along much better than most fathers and sons could ever hope to.

After a moment Jennifer Sheffield turned to Noel. "What I'd like to know is why the sudden interest in my dollhouses? You've made the rounds of all three of them this evening."

Noel grinned. He should have known she'd notice. "Because, Mother, I've met a young woman who shares your love of the same hobby." He'd told Natalia at the café on Thanksgiving that he was going to tell his parents about her, but he hadn't.

His feelings for her had been too new for him to share with someone else then.

Jennifer clapped her hands together, then reached for the remote control. She turned the volume down on the Christmas special until only the faint sounds of carols filled the room. "Is she the reason for that special gleam I've seen lurking in your eyes lately?"

"What gleam?" Noel was prepared to tell his parents about Natalia now. But he was going to enjoy watching their curiosity run rampant first.

"As if you have a secret, but one that is too wonderful for you to believe might be true," she replied without pause.

Noel laughed. "You know me too well, Mother. But it gets even better, especially from your standpoint."

"What do you mean?"

"She's a Christian. I mean a Christian like you and Dad are Christians."

"Hallelujah!" his mother sang out. Noel wasn't surprised when he saw tears fill her eyes. She was an emotional woman. "That's an answer to our prayers for you, Son."

Noel's father reached out and placed his hand on his wife's arm. "Now wait a minute, Dear," he said with the steadiness of his legal profession. "Noel didn't say he was marrying her."

"But I'd like to." Noel didn't want to leave any doubt in their minds concerning his intentions toward Natalia. He had the pleasure of seeing shock, unlike any other time before, cover his distinguished father's face. He chuckled. "Dad, I think I've finally gotten the last word." That was a joke between them. Quincy Sheffield was a brilliant man, and it was a rare moment when someone said anything that could close his mouth.

The older man, whose appearance was a good indication of how Noel would look in thirty years, chuckled back. "Most definitely," he conceded before his face turned serious. "But if she is, as you say, a Christian, who holds Christ as the center of her life, then I'm sorry, Son, but—" He paused and looked at his wife.

Her joy seemed to wilt like a flower left without water on a hot summer day, though with a nod she encouraged him to continue.

"What, Dad?"

His father turned back to him. "I'm sorry, Son, but I doubt she'll marry you without your being one as well."

Noel walked over to the dogs and, kneeling down, patted the head of the older German shepherd. Laddie responded with his happy-go-lucky doggie grin and his tail tapping happily against the floor. Noel smiled at the dog, then stood and faced his parents.

"She took me to see the oratorio *Messiah*, by George Handel, the other night. To say I was emotionally moved would be a gross understatement." He paused and looked up toward the star that twinkled on top of the tree. It made him remember the star it signified. The star that heralded the birth of God's Son on earth, the star that told the world that a whole new volume in the world's story was starting.

He looked back at his parents and smiled. "What I experienced," he said, "was something almost life changing. No." He corrected himself. "It *was* life changing. During that performance, I realized I wanted all the promises of those fantastic, prophetic words. I wanted to believe everything. And you know what, Mom?" He looked at his mother, then turned to his father. "Dad? I do. I might not know much, but I believe. I believe with all my heart that it's true—that Jesus is God's Son, that He is God."

"Hallelujah!" his father's voice sang out.

Noel saw tears come into his father's eyes, but he wasn't concerned. They weren't the sad ones of the only other time he had seen them in his strong father's eyes: the day they had buried the wonderful woman who had given Noel life. These tears were happy ones. And with his limited understanding Noel could grasp why his father felt so moved that tears would fill his eyes now.

"Tell us about her," his mother whispered, dabbing at the corners of her own eyes. "Tell us about this woman we've been praying for many years would enter your life."

"You've been praying for her?"

She nodded. "We suspected that only a woman you loved would be able to lead you to Christ."

"That's why we've been, well, leaving you alone," his father added.

"We always hoped that such a woman would come into your life and share her faith with you," his mother explained.

"That's the truth," his father agreed.

"Natalia is wonderful and—" He stopped speaking when he saw his parents' faces turn ashen. "What?"

"*Natalia* is the girl's name?" His father reached over and took his wife's hand.

The atmosphere in the room changed from joy to apprehension. Noel felt the muscles along his shoulders tense and forced himself to relax.

"Natalia Pappas—"

His mother gasped, and Noel stopped speaking. She

seemed to wilt against his father while her slender white hands covered her face. His father cradled her against him.

Noel was at a loss. Then his mother lowered her hands from her face, and he saw a rapturous expression coloring her features.

"Has she. . .by any chance. . .mentioned to you whether she was adopted?" she asked.

Noel frowned. "Adopted?" An uneasy feeling ran through him. "No. She's never said anything to me about being adopted. The only thing I know is that she loves her family very much. Her father is a priest—"

His mother's gaze searched his face. "A Greek Orthodox priest? From Greece?"

"How—?" He held out his hands in question.

For a moment it was almost as if he weren't there. His mother turned to his father, and Noel heard the older man say, "All in God's timing, my dear. It's all in His hands."

She nodded, and her soft, platinum blond curls bobbed silkily against her shoulders. "That's what you've always told me, my dear, wise husband. And it seems you have been correct."

Ordinarily Noel wouldn't interrupt such a moment between his parents, but he had to know what they were talking about. It concerned Natalia. "What's 'all in God's timing'? What's 'in His hands'?"

The older Sheffield narrowed his eyes, silently asking his wife for permission to tell. She nodded slightly, and his father turned to him. "You recall we told you that before your adoptive mother and I met, she gave birth to a little girl. What we haven't told you is that she deserted the little girl in a bus station in a small city in Greece on Christmas Eve nearly twenty-five years ago. We've been praying for the little girl every day since we met. A Greek Orthodox priest and his wife adopted her. She was born on December 1, the same day as you, my son, three years later. That little girl, Natalia Pappas, grew into a young woman who models under the name Audrey Shepherd."

Except for the clock striking the hour of ten and the soft breathing of the dogs, silence reigned after his father stopped speaking.

Noel knew he was staring at his parents.

His mouth hung open.

But he couldn't help it.

Never in his wildest imaginings would he have considered such an amazing story as his father had just described. The fact that his adoptive mother had given up a baby, when she herself had been little more than a child, wasn't news to him. His parents had never made a secret of the life she had led before she met his father and, more importantly, before she met the Lord Jesus Christ. Both occurred at about the same time.

No.

What astonished Noel was that the little girl his father referred to, and the woman he had thought about since the first time he had seen her looking at the Rockefeller Center Christmas tree three years earlier, were one and the same. Natalia!

He smiled at his parents to ease their minds in case they were wondering how he felt. And the thought kept playing through his head: The Supreme Being had been orchestrating the events of their lives as much as the conductor had orchestrated the *Messiah*.

"Hallelujah!" Noel finally managed to whoop out. He reached for his parents and engulfed them in a gigantic hug.

The three stood together and laughed with relief, joy, and thanksgiving. Then, in the twinkling lights of the Christmas tree, with the soft strains of carols playing inside and the snow falling gently to the earth outside, they cried happy tears.

❧

Natalia looked away from the slow-burning fire to the Charles X clock on the mantel in the Howards' living room as it struck ten o'clock. She sighed. The sound of Christmas carols from the special the Howards were watching on TV and the softly falling snow lit by streetlights outside the huge window gave a cozy feeling to the night. It was a moment of family comfort, one Natalia treasured to have found in New York City. Kneeling down, she rubbed her fingers absently across Prince's velvety ears. The dog lifted his head, seemed to smile, yawned, then lowered his head to the carpet. Prince liked a warm place to lie down and a thick carpet beneath him.

Only one thing would make this moment more perfect, Natalia thought. And that would be to have Noel by her side. She sighed as she looked out the window again. That wouldn't happen for a few days. She had to go to Maine on a modeling shoot early the next morning and wouldn't return until the following week.

"You really like him, don't you?" Janet Howard asked from her place on the sofa.

Natalia looked over at her. "Who? Prince? Of course I do."

"Oh, darling girl! Don't you think I know you well enough to know when you sigh over your dog and when you sigh over the man you—love?" she asked. Her husband chuckled softly.

"She has a point," Jasper Howard agreed with his wife, tilting his recliner forward.

Natalia knew what that meant. He was ready for a serious discussion.

Her gaze went back and forth between the two people she loved as much as she did her own family. She knew they wouldn't be put off. She was glad. She wanted to tell them. "I do. . .love. . .him," she admitted. She let the smile in her soul shine out and laughed. "I do!"

Janet clapped her hands together. "It's like a fairy-tale romance."

"It is!" How many times had she herself used that expression? "Made even more wonderful because the prince of my dreams wants to welcome the Prince of Peace into his life."

"Oh, darling girl!" Janet exclaimed.

"That's wonderful," Jasper said.

"I was going to ask about that," Janet admitted. "But I trusted your judgment."

"Just pray for him," Natalia implored. "We haven't really had a chance to discuss it, but I'm certain he made a decision the other night at the *Messiah*." His answer, after she had asked him if everything had changed, *"My darling, I think you might count on it. . ."* had been going through her head like a glorious refrain for the last two days. "He hasn't said anything specifically," she continued, "but I don't think he will until his decision to believe can be justified by his knowledge of who Jesus is."

"Many people need to let their intellect catch up with their belief, especially when it's new and profound," Jasper pointed out. "Don't worry."

"Oh, I'm not," Natalia said, smiling. "I just can't wait for these next few days to pass so we can see each other again. He loves onomastics, the study of names, so I challenged him to discover who Jesus is by studying His names and—"

"That's it!" Janet exclaimed and jumped up, startling both Natalia and Prince. Prince jumped up suddenly too and stood at canine attention while Natalia gathered the pillows that Janet's sudden movement had scattered all over the floor.

"What's 'it'?" Natalia asked, looking at Jasper. His eyes crinkled at their corners. He was used to his wife's sudden movements.

"That's where I've seen him before!" Janet clicked her fingers together. "I *knew* he looked familiar."

Natalia frowned as she instructed Prince to lie back down. "What are you talking about?"

But Janet only waved at her as she dashed over to the bookshelf. "Here it is!" She pulled a book off the shelf. *"What's in a Name?* by Noel Sheffield."

"What?" She reached for the book Janet passed to her. She turned to the back jacket and gasped when Noel's smiling face stared up at her. Rubbing her fingertips over the beloved features, she whispered, "Noel."

" 'Loves onomastics, the study of names,' " Janet repeated. "Darling girl, he's one of the foremost authorities on the meanings of names. Not only that, but this book has been on the *New York Times* best-seller list for weeks. And I think he's had other successful books as well."

"He never said a word."

"Does that bother you?"

Does it? Natalia wondered. She shook her head. "No, it really doesn't. I didn't tell him much about my modeling career. Probably for the same reason he didn't tell me about this. He didn't want me to judge him by it any more than I wanted him to judge me by my modeling." She held up the book. "Is it good?"

"Wonderful," Janet answered. "I bought it in case one of our sons ever decides to make us grandparents. I'll have it ready for them to search out names."

"Umm." Natalia wasn't thinking about Janet's words nor the Howards' married-but-childless sons. She had turned to the beginning of the book Noel had written. It was his thoughts, his words. That made it important to her.

"Why don't you read it?" Janet suggested.

"I think I've already started," she admitted wryly.

Janet and Jasper exchanged amused and knowing glances, then settled back and watched the Christmas special.

"Happy reading," Janet said.

Natalia gladly lowered her gaze to the book.

But out of the corners of her eyes, she saw Jasper wiggle his left ring finger with his wedding band glistening around it, then motion to her. Janet nodded and smiled. Natalia knew they thought wedding bells might soon be pealing for her.

Natalia hoped they were right.

æ

"I still don't see how you could have kept from going to her and telling her everything once you found out she was living here in New York," Noel said for about the tenth time to his parents.

The Christmas special had ended long ago, although, after his parents' revelations, no one had paid any attention to it. The three were sitting around the fireplace talking. They had a lot to talk about.

"I wanted to," his mother admitted. "Oh, how I yearned to. But after much prayer I didn't think it was right. Maybe if I'd put her in an orphanage, I would have gone to her. But, Noel, I had deserted her in a bus station and in a foreign country. It would be difficult for anyone to forgive another person for that, especially the person who had given you life." She shrugged her shoulders, reminding Noel of Natalia. "It goes against even the most primitive laws of how a mother is to act toward her child."

"Mom." Noel squeezed his mother's hand. "I know Natalia. She will forgive you. In fact, I'm sure she already has without knowing you."

"But, from what you've said, she hasn't even mentioned she was adopted."

"That's true. But I don't think it's a reflection on you as much as a reflection on how much she loves the family that raised her. She loves them dearly."

"I am so glad for that, so thankful," his mother said. Noel could feel the truth of that declaration. It radiated from her.

"Please let me handle introducing the two of you," he said.

His mother beamed at him. "Would you do that for me?"

"Of course, Mom. What do you think? I have no choice really. I love both of you. I now know something that concerns Natalia in a very personal way." He paused. "Other than that, would you understand me if I said it's something I feel led to do?"

His parents nodded.

"God's leading," his father said, his voice filled with emotion. "It's a wonderful gift God gives a believer in His Son, Jesus, by the Holy Spirit."

Noel nodded. "I have a lot to consider the next few days while Natalia is away on her photo shoot." He had already told them she would be in Maine for the next several days. "Not only do I have to consider how I will tell her what you've told me about her parentage, but I have an assignment from Natalia too. She's charged me with learning about Jesus through studying His names."

His mother gasped. "Oh!" She hopped up from her chair like a surprised cat and dashed over to the tree. Kneeling down, she rummaged through the gaily wrapped presents until she found one. Coming back to Noel, she held it against her chest for a moment. "I ordered this several weeks ago. It arrived today." She handed it to him. "Please open it now."

Noel glanced over at his father, who shrugged his shoulders.

He gave his attention to the Christmas gift paper that covered the book. The Christ child was depicted on it. He rubbed his fingers over the golden image. *"For he shall reign for ever and ever!"* He didn't think he would ever look at manger scenes again without the music from the *Messiah* going through his head and thrilling his soul. He removed the paper carefully. It was his turn to gasp when the title of the book was revealed to him.

The Names of Jesus.

He looked up at his mother and didn't try to hide the tears that had gathered in his eyes. "You. . .and your. . .daughter—" He paused. "You and Natalia are so much alike, Mother." He looked down at the book again. "What a coincidence."

"Son." His father rested his large hand upon Noel's shoulder. "You will soon find that with God"—the older man cleared his throat—"there are no coincidences."

Noel nodded. That was something he was fast learning.

eleven

Natalia arrived at her apartment at 10:00 P.M. the following Tuesday night. The phone rang one minute later.

She answered it, and Noel's voice greeted her. "I'm glad you're back in town," he said.

She took off her coat, flipped on the tree-lights switch with her toe, and plopped down on the sofa to gaze out at the flurries of snow that danced among the trees in the park across the avenue.

"Me too," she responded. "I missed you."

"Not nearly as much as I missed you."

She pushed her hair behind her ear and smiled into the phone. "That's debatable."

"Well, how about we debate it tomorrow?"

"When and where?"

"Central Park. Noon. By the statue of Balto."

She laughed. "I think you've set me up."

"That's only the start. I have a very special Christmas surprise for you."

"But it's not Christmas yet." They still had a week to go before that blessed day arrived.

"Ah, dear Natalia, I'm beginning to think that Christmas, for those who believe, is an event to be celebrated every day."

"Noel—" she whispered then hesitated. "Does this mean—?"

"Tomorrow," he interrupted her. "You told me the first day

141

we spoke that you believe in something similar to fairy tales, what you called 'God tales.'"

The delight she felt at his words made her weak. She was glad she was sitting.

"Well, let me organize tomorrow. Trust me and"—he paused and his voice lowered—"trust God. It will be a day you won't ever forget. I promise you. A day that will change your life, mine, and probably several others' forever."

She squeezed her eyes shut. She was sure he was going to tell her he believed, and then he was going to ask her to marry him. She knew what her answer would be. It was a fairy-tale romance, made perfect because her prince had finally discovered why he liked the Christmas season so much and let the Spirit of God—not just the Christmas spirit—work in his heart.

"Okay. Tomorrow. Noon. By the statue of Balto."

"Good night, my love," he whispered.

After they hung up she looked down at her dog. Why did Noel want to meet by the statue of Balto? It had been built to commemorate the brave dog that had led the last relay team of sled dogs over treacherous terrain in 1925 to bring antitoxin to the stricken people of Nome, Alaska.

She shrugged her shoulders. It might be a strange place for a man to propose marriage, but she didn't care.

Kneeling, she rubbed her hand through the soft fur of her tired dog. Prince loved traveling. But after being transported first by helicopter, then plane, then car, he was ready to rest. "Sleep well, Prince Charming, my boy!" Natalia sang out. "For tomorrow we're going to see Prince Charming, the man of my dreams!"

After being away from each other the last four days, Natalia was glad to see Noel waiting for her by the statue. Snow from the previous night still spotted the ground and clung to Balto's curly tail. She detached Prince's lead from his collar and watched her beloved canine friend dart over to Noel.

Feeling jealous, Natalia ran too. Noel lifted her off her feet and twirled her around in his arms. Crystal flakes of snow flittered around them as Noel's lips touched hers. Even though the day was cold, Noel's lips were warm and welcoming.

The kiss ended much too soon for Natalia. But sensing he would soon speak words that would enable them to have a life together, she stood back and looked up at him, leaving her hands locked around his neck.

"I've missed you, and I have so much to tell you," he said, his blue eyes vibrant with a clear light that seemed to originate in his soul.

"Tell! Tell!" She could hardly wait.

"You aren't curious, are you?" he asked and laughed, a deep, rich sound that reverberated around the bare trees, filling the air with joy and her with warmth.

"I am!" she admitted and laughed too. She felt as free and happy as she had when she was a child. "I want to know what happened to you the night of the performance of the *Messiah*. What did you mean when you told me I might count on everything having changed for you? And I want to know why you believe Christmas should be celebrated every day." She let go of him and climbed onto the rocky outcropping on which Balto's statue stood. She wrapped her arms around the statue as she had her own dog so many times. "And I want to know why you wanted to meet here." She stood up straight. "I love this spot and what this statue represents, canines who have given so much in service to humans." She looked at Prince, who was playing in the snow in the clearing to their right. He had served her on a daily basis by offering her unconditional protection, companionship, and love. "But I'm intrigued as to why you chose it. I know you have a good reason."

He stepped up beside her and laid his hand on the ears of the stone dog, worn smooth by children rubbing them for more than seventy-five years. Natalia had often thought people were trying to resurrect the dog, rubbing it like Aladdin's magic lamp, yearning for the same goodness. But if they had only known much more remarkable goodness and truth could be theirs simply by believing in the redemptive work of Jesus, the Man who was resurrected.

That thought brought all others to a stop.

She guessed, even before Noel spoke, that that was the reason he'd wanted to meet here.

He must have seen the resemblance between Balto and his teammates' heroic drive in the dead of an Alaskan winter to save the people of Nome and that of the much greater redemptive work of the Lord Jesus Christ who came to earth to save humanity with the medicine He brought for sin: His own death and resurrection.

"Did you know it took twenty mushers and that many teams of dogs to carry antitoxin to the people of Nome, Alaska, who were dying from diphtheria?" Noel began speaking without preamble. He patted the dog, who had been about the same size as Prince. "And that Balto was the lead dog who got them through, using his God-instilled instincts in the blizzard during those last crucial miles into town?"

She nodded. She knew but didn't want to interrupt what Noel was saying.

"I've known it too, since I was a little boy." He indicated the shiny ears. "I helped polish them by touching them so much when I was a boy. Whenever I could I came here." He sighed. "Like who Santa Claus represented, I loved this dog and what he symbolized." He jumped down and pointed to the plaque in front of the dog.

" 'Dedicated to the indomitable spirit of the sled dogs that relayed antitoxin six hundred miles over rough ice across treacherous waters through arctic blizzards from Nenana to the relief of stricken Nome in the winter of 1925.' "

He was silent for a moment; it seemed to Natalia as if the angels in God's heaven waited with her for Noel's next words.

"The night of the performance I finally started to realize that a rescue mission was exactly what Jesus did for the town of earth by coming to us as a baby. It was something much more grand than what God's creatures and the men who drove them did for the town of Nome all those years ago."

"Hallelujah," she whispered.

In the space between the snowflakes falling around them, she was certain she heard angels sing out the same word of praise.

"I used to think that if Jesus had been anything more than a good man or a prophet, He would have taken the misery and pain out of the world. But I finally realized that His coming to earth as fully Man and fully God, more than two thousand years ago, was just part of the story. A climax in the story of God's redemption of mankind, to be sure," he added, "but only part of the story."

He gazed into her eyes deeply, and Natalia saw the love of

a man for a woman—for her—shining out of his eyes. It was a love she readily recognized because she had seen it often between people she cared a great deal about: her parents, Stavros and Allie, her married brothers and sister, Janet and Jasper. But to see it directed toward her, a true love—not one of infatuation or for the beauty of her outward self—was an experience that nearly took her breath away. His next words did that, however, for what he said had maturity to it, an unusual understanding for a new believer.

"I finally realized we are only partway through the Book—that the patriarchs, judges, kings, and prophets of the Old Testament, the birth of Christ, even the church, are part of the story. They are climaxes in the novel, but not *the* climax. That climax will be when Christ returns. That will be the 'happily ever after' of the story. Sickness and pain will be no more, and the heavenly choir of angels as well as believers will sing, ' "He will reign for ever and ever!" ' " His eyes widened in joy. "And you know what, Natalia? Both of our voices will now be part of that choir."

"Oh, Noel!" She pulled him to her. "I am so glad. So glad."

"Wait. There's more."

"What else could there be?"

"You'd be surprised," he replied in a way that perplexed her. "First, did you know there are more than a hundred names for Jesus? That's because not one name, or even three, can contain all of who He is."

"Noel! How did you start studying them? Using the *Messiah* as a guide?"

He moved over to the rock outcropping, sat down, and pulled her onto his lap. She felt warm and wonderful and cherished, everything a woman sitting upon a man's lap on a cold December day could want to feel. "Well, now, here's something amazing."

"Something else, you mean?"

He rubbed his nose against hers. "So many great things have happened the last few days."

"Tell me," she prompted. "I promise not to interrupt."

He laughed. "Is that possible?"

She laughed too.

"Well, when I told my mother about your having advised me to learn about Jesus by studying His names, she gave me a gift she had oddly bought for me this Christmas—a book called *The Names of Jesus*. I thought at first it was a coincidence."

Natalia was about to tell him she didn't believe in coincidences when he seemed to pull the words right out of her mouth.

"Of course, I now understand that nothing is happenstance. God had your advice and my mother's gift coordinated."

"Coordinated. Hmm. I like that." She had never heard it put that way, but she thought it perfect. She could see that Noel would add fantastic thoughts to a believer's efforts to understand God. Life with him would be an adventure.

She paused. If he ever offered to share his life with her.

But when would she hear the words from his mouth?

He leaned toward her until his forehead came down to touch hers, then moved his head back a fraction of an inch. "I still have more to tell you, things I've—recently—learned." He hesitated over the words, and she felt fingers of apprehension move up her spine.

"What things do you have to tell me?" She thought he was referring to his career as a writer. But he said things he'd recently learned.

He glanced at his watch. "I'll tell you on our way."

"On our way?" She looked at him, even more puzzled now. "On our way where?"

"To meet my parents."

twelve

Arm in arm, talking and laughing the entire way, Noel and Natalia walked across the park to the garage close to Noel's brownstone town house where he kept his cars: a Jeep and a red sports car. Since the weather was inclement and Prince was with them, he pulled out his Jeep. After awhile of Noel maneuvering the Jeep across Manhattan's busy streets, Natalia turned to him with a grin. "So when were you going to tell me about your publishing success?"

He grimaced. "How did you—?" he started to ask then stopped. "Actually I was going to tell you about it today." He glanced over at her as they drove onto the George Washington Bridge. "Are you upset?"

She offered him her hand, and he took it. "I hardly have the right, Noel, since I didn't tell you the extent of my modeling career, did I?"

"Being a writer isn't who I am—"

"Any more than being a model is who I am."

"Exactly."

She was glad they agreed.

"It's a wonderful book," she said as they crossed over the state line and into New Jersey.

The corners of his mouth turned up in surprise. "You've read it?"

"Uh-huh, a few nights ago. Janet Howard had a copy. That's how I found out."

"I think the next one will deal with the names of Jesus found in the *Messiah*."

"Noel!" she exclaimed. "That's wonderful."

"No," he corrected her. *"He's* wonderful."

She certainly wouldn't deny that. "But on a human level you are too, my love. You are a wonderful counselor. Look at what you've done for Rachel."

"Me?" His glance left the road for a second to meet her steady and open gaze. "Don't you mean *you?*" he corrected her.

"I haven't done much," she demurred. "Just talked to her by phone a couple of times."

" 'Haven't done—'? Natalia, giving the girl your personal number and allowing her to call you is—"

"Just trying to be a good steward with what God has given me, Noel," she finished for him. "If the profession in which I make my livelihood can help somebody simply by its nature and by the way I live my life within it"—she shrugged— "then that gives my work real worth."

"Well, the example of your life has turned Rachel's around. She doesn't wear skimpy clothes to school anymore, she's cleaned up her speech, and I don't think she'll lead a wild life any longer. Her parents don't think so either, and they couldn't be happier." He drew in a deep and satisfied breath. "They were so concerned about her and didn't know what else to do. That was why they asked me to help her as much as I could in my capacity as her high school counselor. It's so rewarding to see that family drawing together."

"I'm so glad for them. And of course you must know she's not pregnant. It was a false alarm."

"But one that God used in His plan for her."

Natalia let her gaze roam over his profile. He had chiseled

male features that appeared to be cast in bronze as he concentrated on both the road and his thoughts. But she knew what warmth was there, that of a man who cared about a young high school student, about his own family, about her, and now about the things of God. The degree of his understanding amazed her. Seldom did a person come to believe and learn so quickly. But he had been around parents who believed all his life. That had to have made a difference. "You're absolutely correct," she agreed after a moment and turned her gaze forward as the jeep ate up the miles. She felt such contentment. Her world seemed to be falling into shape perfectly.

"If only *my* mother had had a role model like you to talk to when she was young," he continued after several minutes of companionable silence. "She might not have become wild."

Her glance slid to his face again. "Your mother was wild?" She knew from earlier conversations that his mother was a strong Christian.

"Well," he replied, "my biological mother was a very strong Christian. My father has laughingly told me in the past that she probably never did anything wrong in her entire life."

"Your *'biological*—'?" Her eyes widened. "You mean the woman you refer to as your mother is your *stepmother?*"

"No, she's actually my mother too," he stated. "She adopted me legally when I was nine."

"I had no idea." But as with his being a writer and her, a high-fashion model, she wondered what else they might have neglected to share with one another. She had never told him she had been adopted either, but only because the subject had never come up. And even though her father had encouraged her to be open to finding her biological mother, she had given the situation to God on her first day back in

New York from Kastro, and she really didn't think about it. At some point she knew she must tell Noel. But right now he was telling her about himself. And there was no way she was going to interrupt that.

"It isn't something that's in my mind. I remember my biological mother with much fondness and love, but Jennifer *is* my mother."

"I can understand that." *Could she ever!*

"I imagine you can," he said evenly.

She looked at him sharply. Did he know about her having been adopted? Or was he simply referring to her being able to empathize with him? But as the car covered the miles across New Jersey on the way to his parents' home, he continued to talk about his family, so she decided to let it go. She had plenty of time to tell her story.

"My natural mother died when I was six. Remember the conversation we had about Santa Claus at the café the day of the parade?"

Surprise flickered across her face. Santa Claus? What did Santa have to do with this? "Yes?"

"Well, I finally figured out a few days ago that one reason I was so negative about letting my parents teach me about God was because I was angry about the death of both my mother and, as strange as it might sound, Santa. Finding out Santa wasn't real, he didn't live at the North Pole, and he didn't fly through the sky with a sleigh full of toys every Christmas Eve was very traumatic for me. It was almost as if he had died too."

Her heart went out to the hurting little boy Noel had been. In Kastro, little Jeannie Andreas had been wounded in a similar way by her mother's desertion of her. But at least Natalia had been able to hug the little girl close to her and do fun things with her to try to ease her pain. Then Jeannie's new mother, Allie, had come into her life and filled it with the mother's love the little girl had so craved. But Natalia couldn't do anything for the boy Noel had been. She could only be thankful for the new mother who had adopted him—the boy who had grown into the man she loved—when he was nine.

"That's one of the dangers associated with the secular myth about Santa." Her answer was soft but firm in its psychological affirmation of what had happened to him. "What concerns many is that kids are taught to believe in Santa and his powers, rather than being taught that the true Santa Claus was a Christian, who believed in Christ with his whole heart. Children are given a tarnished and untrue image of Christ to believe in, as a sort of Christmas spirit, rather than the real God. All these things would, I think, make that dear old clergyman Nicholas from the Greek world long ago very sad."

"You know, Natalia, I can remember crying out to both Jesus and Santa to save my mother." There was a steely quality to his voice as he thought back. She reached over and placed her hand over his. Instinctively his hand grasped hers. "When neither did, I decided they were both fake."

"But, Noel, just because Jesus didn't save your mother—"

His hand tightened on hers before he let go of it to take the exit ramp off the interstate. "I know that now. But try getting that into the head of an angry six year old who just lost the most important person in his life, as well as the Santa he thought could give him his wish for Christmas— his mother's health." He turned into a gated roadway and pulled the car to the side. He cut the engine, and peace enveloped the car. Only the sound of Prince's breathing could be heard in the hushed world that surrounded them.

Natalia gazed out on one of the most beautiful wintertime vistas she'd ever seen. A Currier and Ives print couldn't have painted the snow-covered world any better. Rolling hills, distant barns, stately homes, the bare branches of trees silhouetted against the horizon, and a few brave conifers holding out their needle-clothed arms, filled the white world of earth and sky. It was still and wearing its snow mantle, perfect and pure.

Noel turned to her and took her hand in his again. His fingers were warm, firm, sure. "I know I'll see my mother again because of what God, born as a baby, did for us all. And in Jennifer I was given a wonderful second mother."

"From how you've talked about her, it's obvious you love her very much."

"I do. She's a very special woman."

Natalia thought that now was the time to tell him about her own background. It wasn't important to her because she had always considered *Mamma* and *Baba* her very own parents, but she knew she had to tell Noel. Whether she wanted it or not, her biological parentage was part of who she was. She leaned toward him and placed her hand on his cheek.

"That's something I can understand, Noel." She was silent for a moment. "You see, I was adopted too, by both of my parents. I never knew my natural mother or father."

When he didn't respond, by word or even a flicker of emotion in his face, she felt apprehension slicing through her again.

Finally he admitted in a low and husky tone, "I know you were adopted, Natalia."

Then fear ran in to keep her apprehension company.

That was the last thing she'd expected. Her hand fell from his face, and she sat back. *How did he know?* "You know? Did the Howards tell you?" That would be the only way he could have known. Not even the tabloids had that information.

"No. My father told me a few days ago."

"Your father?" Now panic ran through her system like a fire alarm might a building.

"Until then I had no idea of what I'm about to tell you."

"Noel." She hugged herself, rubbing her hands against her arms. She could feel the goose bumps rising beneath her cashmere sweater. "You're scaring me. How could your father have known?" Then suspicion filled her. "Have you had me investigated?" She nearly choked on the word and reached for Prince who, picking up on her fear, had stuck his head into the front of the Jeep. His great head, with its mouth full of teeth, was between her and Noel. She was unexpectedly glad she had her trusted canine companion with her.

Dear Lord! Have I been wrong to trust Noel? To love him? She cried out to God, the One who would always be with her and could always be counted upon.

"No," a voice spoke calmingly within her. *"Everything is in My control. Just trust."*

"I know this seems strange to you—"

"Strange!" Her voice shook. "Noel, how do you know—?"

"I know because Jennifer, the woman my father married when I was nine, was a very wild teenager. More so than Rachel. And, unlike Rachel, when my adoptive mother was sixteen, she did become pregnant. Then, when she was seventeen, she was backpacking around Greece with her boyfriend—"

"Greece!" Natalia gasped. *I know! I know what Noel is about to say.*

She saw him reach for her, but she barely felt his arms as they wrapped around her. She went numb and had to force herself to hear his words through the pounding in her brain.

"—when she gave birth to a baby girl."

'Gave birth to a baby girl!'

As if a gigantic vacuum had pushed its way into her chest, Natalia's breath was sucked out of her. It would have been easier for her to understand if Noel had announced he was going to take a trip to the moon rather than grasp the words he'd just uttered.

"I—was—that—baby?" She finally managed to gulp enough air to ask against his shoulder. Tears flooded her eyes at the unexpected wave of euphoria that washed over her upon discovering her mother's whereabouts. She had always been so blasé about meeting her biological mother. Suddenly she realized her cool indifference had been a facade. Now it was melting like an ice sculpture under the warm rays of the sun. And she knew her *baba* had been right to encourage her to meet her natural mother someday.

She heard answering tears in Noel's voice. "Yes, you, my darling. My adoptive mother—is your biological mother. She gave birth to you in Greece—on December first—three years to the day—after I was born." Emotions clogged his throat, halting his speech.

For a moment they held one another, and Natalia knew the arms holding her were the ones she wanted around her—*"for better or for worse, for richer or for poorer, in sickness and in health"*—forever.

His clean masculine scent filled her senses. She was so glad Noel was the man she had thought he was. "My *baba* always encouraged me to find my biological mother, or at least be receptive to her finding me," she whispered.

He moved just far enough back from her on the leather seat so he could look into her eyes. "Really?"

She nodded.

"And are you, my darling? Receptive to her finding you?" She thought from the way the blue of his eyes became as deep and intense as a mountain lake in winter that it was something for which he fervently hoped.

She wiped the tears from her eyes as the miracle of God's timing swept through her. "It's something I prayed about and gave to God the afternoon we met, Noel. The only other thing I asked of Him—" She stopped speaking as the wonder of it filled her, and she turned her gaze to the pristine world of white that surrounded them.

"What, my darling?"

She turned back to him and, remembering her plea to God, repeated it. "I asked Him, if possible, that my biological mother might be a Christian now," she said softly.

Making a sound of joy, he pulled her close to him and, like leaves rustling on the ground, said, "She is, Natalia. Not only that but"—he spoke with more force—"she's been keeping an eye on you through your doorman Roswell for the last five years—ever since she realized the modeling superstar Audrey Shepherd was her daughter."

She blinked. "Roswell?"

He nodded. "She came to your apartment building, and after understanding what sort of man Roswell was, she confided in him. That's why the dear man hasn't retired. He's been staying on for my mother." He gave a small laugh and touched the tip of her nose. "Your mother."

"My mother. . ." *To have a mother again.* It was a gift, especially since she knew what sort of woman she was from hearing Noel talk about her so much.

"But now Roswell will retire and live in the beautiful carriage house on this estate with his wife and family for as long as they wish—now that he no longer needs to give her weekly reports about you. When he met me the morning of our birthdays, he didn't know I was Jennifer Sheffield's son. He just found out yesterday when I told him."

"And your mother—my natural mother—wants to meet me now?"

"With all her heart. And—to ask your forgiveness."

Natalia shook her head. That thought seemed almost absurd to her.

"I've had a wonderful life, Noel. I grew up in a land that seems like something out of a fairy tale with the most wonderful family imaginable. Then God brought me to America, and I've lived like a princess in a storybook. And now the man I love, the prince of my dreams"—she ran her hand over the fine contours of his face—"has not only discovered the Prince of Peace but has welcomed Him into his life." She shook her head. "No, Noel, I don't have to forgive my natural mother for anything. I only have to thank her. I would not ask for a different life."

"Natalia," he whispered and pulled her close to him. "Dear Natalia. That mind of yours keeps up with your heart in a way I wouldn't have believed possible"—he leaned back and held her face between his hands—"if I hadn't lived with Jennifer for nearly twenty years. She has filled my world with the same mature wisdom. You and she walked different paths— something unusual for mothers and daughters to do—and yet

God has brought you both to the same blessed one. You are so much alike. It is—" He stopped what he was going to say. "Well, it *would* be unbelievable if I didn't understand how the Great Conductor works."

Natalia nodded. "Amazing, isn't it?"

"More like miraculous."

She laughed lightly, thrilled to hear Noel speak in such a godly way. "I'll agree with that."

His eyes narrowed. "Are you ready to meet your mother, my darling?"

She nodded slowly. "That is something for which my earthly *baba*, as well as my heavenly Father, have been preparing me for several years. Yes, Noel. I'm ready."

thirteen

To say that Natalia was delighted with the woman who had given her life would be putting it mildly. God had ordained their reunion so there were only tears of joy and much laughter. Natalia felt more like a beloved child coming home after a long absence than a daughter who had been deserted so many years before. If she had been given a choice of any woman in the world to be her biological mother, it would have been Jennifer Sheffield. She loved her mother upon sight, and she knew her mother loved her too, as Jennifer held her and kissed her and explored her face, looking for the infant of so long ago. All the days of their lives they would cherish finding one another after so many years.

The tree lights twinkled, a new snowfall drifted down past the windows, and the three German shepherds lay happily near the fireplace, for Prince had become fast friends with Laddie and his son, Harry. And Noel and his father sat quietly while Natalia and Jennifer held hands and talked about everything—the far distant past and the more recent one.

"You must remember, Natalia, that I was a very foolish young woman," Jennifer said. "To put it succinctly, I was a spoiled brat. I had been given everything money could buy, and I spurned it and the lifestyle it bought for me. But, worst of all, I left you, my precious baby, in a bus station in a foreign land. The only right thing I did was to wait and make sure good people found you. When that wonderful man—

that Greek Orthodox priest—and his wife held you, I knew they would love you and never let you go." She glanced at the older Sheffield and sent him a look of thankfulness. "Until I met Noel's father, I was a very lost, very nasty young woman. Quincy's faith and his love of God got through to me as nothing else could—not the doctors my parents took me to see or the rehab clinics from which I repeatedly escaped."

Natalia squeezed the long and slender hand that so resembled her own. "That's an amazing testimony. . .Mother." The title rolled easily off her lips. She had always called her adoptive mother *Mamma,* so calling her natural mother "Mother" did not conflict with the special relationship she'd had with her *mamma* at all. Natalia knew too that her *mamma* would have been glad.

"Mother?" The older woman squeezed her eyes together. "What have I done that you'd call me that wonderful name?"

"You gave me life," Natalia responded, "and it's a life I've liked very much. Thank you."

"But can you forgive me, dear daughter? Can you ever forgive me for being so immature, so wrong, to leave you behind?"

Natalia was slow to answer. She wanted to do so with care. "By giving me away, I think you gave me the best life you could at that time. To grow up in the loving family you found for me was a rare treasure. Not only is my family very special, but the village where I was raised is too."

"We went to Kastro once," Jennifer confessed and motioned to both Noel and her husband. "The three of us did."

"What?" Natalia and Noel asked in unison and looked at one another in disbelief.

Jennifer nodded and answered Noel. "That's where we went on our honeymoon."

"*Kastro* was where we went?" Noel turned to his father for confirmation.

The older man's smile widened. "That's it."

"I remember the village." Noel squinted, as he seemed to search through his memories. "It was a beautiful place. There was a castle on the top of the mountain and donkeys and chickens and kids. Lots of kids."

"Certainly sounds like Kastro," Natalia said, chuckling. She turned back to Jennifer. "But Noel went with you on your *honeymoon?*"

"I had already left one child behind me," Jennifer said quickly. "I wasn't going to leave another I was blessed to have come into my life."

"They took me with them everywhere," Noel interjected. "That's why I didn't remember Kastro at first. We went to so many places."

"Plus, you were just a little boy of nine," his father pointed out, sounding like a lawyer with a mind for details.

"Did you see me?" Natalia had to know.

A dreamy look came into Jennifer's eyes, and Natalia suspected she was recalling memories she often liked to contemplate. It made Natalia feel very special. "Yes, we saw you. We went to church service Sunday morning. You were there dressed in a little yellow sundress with white flowers and matching yellow ribbons that held your nearly translucent hair back in a ponytail."

"I remember that dress." She did, even though it was long ago. "My sister Martha made it for me. It was one of my favorites."

"You were so happy. So carefree. So loved. Your whole family was there." She laughed. "So many people."

"I have five brothers and sisters, and I think several of them were already married then."

"And your father was such a man of God. I knew that day as I watched you with your family that God had taken my bad actions and brought good out of them."

"Did you talk to my *baba?*"

"No. I couldn't do that to the dear man. I learned that his wife, your mother, was quite sick. You were the apple of his eye. I didn't want to chance scaring him. Plus, how would we have communicated without any misunderstandings? I didn't speak a word of Greek then."

Natalia caught the word "then." " 'Then'? You do now?"

"Malista," Jennifer replied, surprising Natalia with a yes. Greek was not a language many people spoke. She listened as her mother continued to speak in perfect Greek. "I thought if I should ever be blessed to be reconciled to you, I wanted to be able to communicate with you. So I've been studying Greek for years. I didn't know, until you became Audrey Shepherd, that you had learned English so well."

A million words could never have conveyed to Natalia the depth of her biological mother's love for her as that act of learning Greek in the hope of their meeting did. It told its own tale and touched Natalia deeply.

"Fharisto poli, Mother," she said, thanking her mother.

"Parakalo." The older woman responded with "you're welcome." "Your English is superb, Natalia. And with only the barest trace of an accent. Very lovely. How did you learn to speak so well?"

"My parents were certain I was American, even if the American authorities wouldn't acknowledge it."

"The little sleeper I dressed you in and the blanket I wrapped you in were emblazoned with the American flag. I wasn't thinking too clearly back then, but I remember I thought everyone would know from those things that you were American. I also wrote a letter saying you were. But I'm not sure exactly what I wrote. I'd started taking drugs by then."

"Drugs?" To see her, Natalia didn't think it was possible.

An almost haunted look entered Jennifer's eyes. "I was very confused, Natalia, and I did a stupid thing. A woman does not desert her child in a bus station without having major problems. I didn't know what else to do. I was desperate."

Natalia remembered the day she'd met Noel. On her walk to the Rockefeller Center Christmas tree she had been praying about her birth mother. She had wondered what kind of woman would leave her newborn baby in a bus station. And God had told her, *"The desperate kind."* Exactly what her mother was admitting to having been—desperate.

She looked deeply into Jennifer's eyes and, seeing how sad recalling her past made her, decided now wasn't the time to question her further. She would sometime but not today. Those questions could be asked and answered in the days and weeks and years to come. They had time.

She went back to Jennifer's question about her learning to speak English. "In the event I ever searched for my roots, my parents wanted me to be able to speak English well."

"And did you?" Jennifer asked with a degree of yearning in her tone that almost made Natalia feel sad. Particularly since she knew her answer. "Ever want to find your roots, I mean?"

Natalia didn't want to hurt this woman who had been such a wonderful mother to Noel, but she had to be truthful. She spoke softly, tenderly. "Not really. I mean I always wanted to come to America, but—oh, please don't feel bad—I never really felt the need to find my biological parents. Even though it was something my *baba* always encouraged me to do."

"He is a very special man. A man of faith, who, I think, has a great understanding about human nature and need."

Natalia thought about her dear *baba* and all the good he had done for the people in Kastro throughout her life and more. "Yes, he does," she agreed. "I always knew I was adopted." She touched her blond hair. "I looked so different from my brothers and sisters, and my mother was too old to have had children when I came along. I assumed you had given me up for a good reason. That's what my parents told me too. Either you couldn't care for me, or I was an embarrassment to you because you were unmarried, or you were sick. Something." She quickly continued, "I've had a wonderful family. One I thank you for finding for me."

"It was God." Jennifer held her hand upward.

Natalia smiled her agreement. "But when Noel told me you were my natural mother, at that very moment I realized how important it was to have you in my life, how right my *baba* was to encourage me to find you or be open to your finding me. And even though it wasn't something I thought I needed, having you in my life is one of the most important things to me now. I'm so thankful to have met you after twenty-six years."

"Thank you, Natalia," she whispered. "I don't deserve your forgiveness, but I thank you from the very bottom of my heart." She dabbed at the corners of her eyes, then blinked and sent Natalia a bright smile. "I thank God He gave you wisdom not to question my motive in giving you up, as if it had been a reflection upon you. Never that! And I thank God for the wonderful people who raised you to be such a lovely young woman. But mostly, right now, I thank God He has brought us together again."

Leaning toward one another, they fell into a natural embrace. Natalia took a deep breath of the essence of the woman who had given her the gift of life. She smelled of peaches and freshly washed clothing, wholesome and clean. Natalia whispered a prayer of thanksgiving to God for protecting her mother through her wild years. "What about my biological father?" Natalia felt compelled to ask after a moment.

Her mother sat back but still held her hand. Natalia was glad. She didn't want to let go either. "He was as bad as I."

"Did he know about me?"

Jennifer nodded sadly. "He told me to get rid of you."

"So you did." Natalia didn't mean for the words to sound so harsh. She offered a thin smile to soften them.

"Yes, but after you were born. Thank God—and only Him— I at least gave you life. On the first day of Advent. I always loved Christmas." She looked at the tree sparkling from its place near the decorated hearth, and a pensive quality came into her tone. "Even when I was a terrible, disrespectful, immoral young woman, I loved the Christmas season, and I thought it was very special you were born then. That's why I left a note saying exactly when your birthday was. The first day of Advent." She looked over at Noel. "The same as my son's."

"The day my parents found me," Natalia explained, "was Christmas Eve, my *mamma*'s birthday. Her name was Natalia, but she was always called Talia. So I was named for both Christmas and my *mamma*."

Jennifer's mouth formed an O. "Your mother's name was

Natalia?" She laughed. "What an amazing humor our God has to have orchestrated everything so perfectly. For your mother to find you on her birthday, for her name to be Natalia, for the Christmas season to be something that spoke to my hardened heart even then." She shook her head at the miracle of it all. "From reading Noel's book I know Natalia means 'of or relating to Christmas.'"

Noel nodded. "'She who is born at Christmas.' Just like my name means 'born at Christmas.'"

"It is the name I would have chosen for you, Natalia, had I been a responsible mother then."

There was a moment of silence in which Natalia lifted up her thoughts and prayers to God, and the other three people seemed to do the same.

Then Natalia, wanting to know one more thing, asked, "Where is my biological father now?"

A look of sadness crossed Jennifer's face.

"He never changed. He died of a drug overdose a couple of years after you were born. But his parents are still alive. I think meeting you, their granddaughter, would be one of the most wonderful gifts they could ever receive." She turned her head in a searching way. "You inherited your exceptional outward beauty from him." She let her fingertips slide across Natalia's face. "Your fine, high cheekbones, your sparkling blue eyes"—she touched the ends of Natalia's hair—"your true blond coloring. He was a handsome man."

"I always wondered who I looked like." Natalia thought most adopted children wondered that, whether they admitted it or not. It wasn't important, just nice to know.

"Your father. Totally." She sighed. "I don't have any pictures of him, but his parents do. It would do his parents good to meet you. After they saw how my life changed, they've been leaning toward Christianity." She shrugged. "But they haven't been able to let go of the bitterness even after all these years. He was their only child. Someday, when you feel ready, maybe we can invite them over."

"I would be honored."

She nodded. "Tell me about your *baba*. Is he well? And your brothers and sisters?"

That Jennifer should ask about her family cemented the love Natalia already felt for the woman who had given her life. Maybe she hadn't done much more than that in the beginning. But it was more than many received in these modern times. And that was something.

Natalia happily told her about her *baba* and Martha and her brothers and sisters. Jennifer asked if they might call and talk to her *baba*, and even though it was very early in the morning in Greece, Natalia didn't hesitate to call him. This was one phone call her *baba* had been waiting for a very long time.

As it was, he had just returned from church, where he had felt the desire to go and pray. Natalia told him what had just transpired, and the dear man understood.

"Ah." His deep gravelly voice spoke through the wire and satellite to his daughter so far away and yet so very close spiritually. "That's why *O Theos*—God—directed me to get on my knees this morning and pray extra hard for you, *Kali mou kori,* my dear daughter. He knew."

"Malista, Baba, He knew," Natalia agreed. And when she told him that Jennifer had learned Greek, and the reason why, the man was overjoyed to be able to speak to her. Smiling, Natalia handed the phone to Jennifer.

Her mother's first words, with tears of joy and thanksgiving, were, *"Papouli,* thank you so very much for raising Natalia in such a God-centered and wonderful way." Natalia took Noel's hand then and walked with him over to the picture window.

For a few moments they stood and looked out at the pristine world surrounding them. Snow still fell softly, a blanket of righteousness and protection for the winter's night.

"King of Kings and Lord of Lords," Natalia heard Noel whisper by her side.

She turned to him.

He turned to her.

They nodded their heads with a degree of oneness that could come only from an understanding of the words Noel had spoken.

Those words said it all.

Everything.

And using only two of the Lord's names.

But for the couple who believed, those two names were enough.

More than enough for them to build a lifetime of happiness and commitment in a continuing fairy-tale romance that would forever have God at its center.

❧

And, beside his tree at Rockefeller Center on Christmas Eve, on bended knee Noel asked Natalia to be his wife. All were present—Jennifer and Quincy Sheffield, Janet and Jasper Howard, Mary and Roswell Lincoln, and Rachel; and, through the amazing technology of cell phones and computers, Natalia's *baba* and sister Martha and a multitude of friends in Kastro; as well as Prince who, as was his job, watched everything carefully. And they clapped their hands in joy when Natalia, to the sound of church bells ringing and the singing of Christmas carols in New York City, said, "Yes!"

Well, not Prince. He thumped his tail against the pavement and smiled his big doggie grin.

Prince seemed to understand he was soon to see his canine family in Kastro again. By Natalia saying yes, a wedding would be planned. Probably for March. And since *Papouli* would officiate, they would all be flying to Kastro.

Prince thumped his tail harder against the pavement.

That was something that appeared to please him very much.

A Letter To Our Readers

Dear Reader:

In order that we might better contribute to your reading enjoyment, we would appreciate your taking a few minutes to respond to the following questions. We welcome your comments and read each form and letter we receive. When completed, please return to the following:

Fiction Editor
Heartsong Presents
PO Box 719
Uhrichsville, Ohio 44683

1. Did you enjoy reading *A Fairy-Tale Romance* by Melanie Panagiotopoulos?

   ❏ Very much! I would like to see more books by this author!
   ❏ Moderately. I would have enjoyed it more if

   _____

   _____

   _____

2. Are you a member of Heartsong Presents? ❏ Yes ❏ No
   If no, where did you purchase this book? _____

   _____

3. How would you rate, on a scale from 1 (poor) to 5 (superior), the cover design? _____

4. On a scale from 1 (poor) to 10 (superior), please rate the following elements.

   _____ Heroine   _____ Plot
   _____ Hero   _____ Inspirational theme
   _____ Setting   _____ Secondary characters

5. These characters were special because?_____

_____

_____

6. How has this book inspired your life?_____

_____

_____

7. What settings would you like to see covered in future
   Heartsong Presents books? _____

_____

_____

8. What are some inspirational themes you would like to see
   treated in future books? _____

_____

_____

9. Would you be interested in reading other Heartsong
   Presents titles? ❑ Yes ❑ No

10. Please check your age range:
   ❑ Under 18   ❑ 18-24
   ❑ 25-34   ❑ 35-45
   ❑ 46-55   ❑ Over 55

Name_____

Occupation _____

Address _____

City_____ State_____ Zip_____

Christmas Duty

4 stories in 1

Life is never still in the military. Even Christmas is a season of challenge. . .a season of change. This year, several servicemen and women will face a range of life altering experiences.

Will these military personnel find Christmas to be a time of renewed hope? Will they hold on to their faith in the Christmas Child and the Savior who can guide their lives today?

Contemporary, paperback, 352 pages, 5 $^3/_{16}$" x 8"

❤ ❤ ❤ ❤ ❤ ❤ ❤ ❤ ❤ ❤ ❤ ❤ ❤ ❤ ❤

❤ ❤ ❤ ❤ ❤ ❤ ❤ ❤ ❤ ❤ ❤ ❤ ❤ ❤ ❤